ALI SPARKES

NIGHT SPEAKERS

OXFORD
UNIVERSITY PRESS

Turn around! her inner voice yelled. *Look! It's probably not even there now! Look!*

Of course. It was probably nothing more than a shadow and her own imagination.

She looked.

A gurgling scream escaped her throat.

It *was* chasing her, like a billow of black smoke, low above the grass, just a few metres behind her, easily keeping pace, eyes glowing. She could hear it *breathing*. She could hear it *laughing*. That was when she knew she would die.

CHAPTER 1

Elena woke up at 1.34 a.m. She didn't need to check the alarm clock on the bedside table. She knew it was 1.34 a.m. It was always 1.34 a.m.

This was the seventh night in a row, and it was getting to be almost normal.

She prodded the button on the clock anyway, and its dim blue light showed **1.34** in blocky digital numbers across the glass. 'Hello again, one thirty-four,' she mumbled. She got up. There was no point staying in bed and trying to get back to sleep; this she had also learned over the past week.

She opened her door without making a sound and slipped downstairs to the kitchen. Since night three she had been getting a hot drink and taking it back up to her room with a couple of biscuits. Then she would sit by her window and consume them, watching the silent, shadowy street below. It was reassuring somehow—making a normal routine out of something so weird.

The first night was nothing that strange, of course. Everyone got insomnia once in a while, didn't they? She had woken up at 1.34 a.m and then been unable to get back to sleep until around six. By breakfast she was groggy but not too tired for school. She hadn't even mentioned it to Mum.

The next night was when it started to get weird. Her eyes pinged open at 1.34 a.m. again. Even then, she wasn't sure it was the same time; the exact same time, to the minute. She really only noticed *that* the third night. But maybe she noticed the song that second night . . . maybe not. It was hard to be sure.

By now, though, sitting at the window on night seven, she knew it all. The time was always 1.34 a.m. exactly and what shoved her so abruptly out of sleep was something like a song. In her dreams there was a long, chiming note like someone sliding a metal spoon down an ancient bell, then a swell of . . . a voice? Was it a voice? It seemed like something singing. A dark and yet somehow golden song that rushed along like a river . . . a thin, straight river . . . a channel of vibrating dark golden song, fizzing and bubbling and beautiful.

'Will you shut up?' she said, out loud. The talking to herself had started on night five. As long as she didn't shout she knew she couldn't be heard. Mum slept like the dead. 'Seriously . . . it's just a sound in your head. Like . . . that ear thing . . . tinnitus or something. It's nothing mystical or sinister. And 1.34 a.m. is probably just when some big machine starts up over on the industrial estate. Or at the power station. Something is making a noise and you're hearing it in your sleep and you're waking up. That's all.'

So why can't you still hear it once you're awake? asked the argumentative imp who plagued these nights by the window.

'It's short. It's gone by the time I sit up,' she explained.

OK—and why can't you just drop back off to sleep again?

'I don't know. I'm just stressed, I guess. Early hours waking—that's a classic symptom of anxiety. I know. I looked it up on the internet.'

Seven nights in a row . . . ? REALLY? Do 13-year-olds usually get that stressed? Is this normal?

She'd looked it up online. She'd typed in 'Why do I keep waking up at the same time each night?' A lot of suggestions came back: noisy neighbours, a gas boiler starting up on a timer, hormonal activity, pets, poltergeists, trapped wind . . .

She knew that it was nothing to do with any of the stuff she had read online. It was something else. Something *very* else. Maybe in the morning she would talk to Mum. Maybe. If Mum seemed OK; if she was having a good day.

Elena settled back into her chair and put her bare feet on the windowsill. On the street below a fox trotted along the pavement, pausing to sniff at the wheelie bins. It cast a long shadow under the dim street lights. Elena called it Velma because she thought it was probably a vixen. She'd seen it several times now. Three of those times it had paused and seemed to stare right up at her for a few seconds, before trotting away on its own business.

3

The terraced houses opposite seemed to stare back at her, their windows like dark, blank eye sockets. She opened her own window and breathed in the night air. It was sweet and cool, full of late May blossom and recently drenched gardens. It had been raining when she'd gone to bed at ten. Clouds drifted across the scattering of stars above, tinged with orange from the distant lights of the industrial estate. The town's street lights were energy-saving blue, but Quarry End remained defiantly lit by tall orange lamps that stayed on all night, fighting off the shadow of the broken hillside that loomed over it. The orange glow seeped across the sky towards the quiet suburban streets where Elena lived, two or three kilometres away.

She picked up a book and settled down at the window to read the night away. A bit of Cathy Cassidy would pass the time, and then she could get into bed with the dawn chorus to sing her to sleep. She might get another hour in before the alarm went off.

Maybe she fell asleep then; maybe she didn't. All she remembered later, in one of those stuttering leaps of time she kept getting, was that her forehead was against the window again, and the night beyond the thin glass seemed to be dissolving through it like tears through tissue.

And standing quite still in the street below was a solitary, misty figure, pointing a gun at her.

CHAPTER 2

It was on the fourth morning that Matt's dad slammed him up against the wall and demanded answers.

'What's going on? You getting help? You got some little scheme going? You trying to mess with me?'

Matt tried to push him away, but he was big and heavy and as solid as a bulldog. He looked a lot like a bulldog too, his jowls hanging and his eyelids sagging at the corners, his brown eyes small and shiny.

'I told you!' Matt shouted, trying to out-blare his old man. 'I got up early! That's all. I've done three cars already. You should be pleased.'

'Why? Why are you getting up early?' said his father, giving him a little shake and blast of stale whisky. 'What are you up to?'

Matt felt tiredness suddenly wash over him like a wave, tugging him down into its undertow, drowning him. 'I don't know why,' he muttered, sagging in his father's grip. 'I just keep waking up and not being able to get back to sleep.'

Something in his face must have rung true because he found himself released and sliding slowly down the rough breeze-block wall. His dad wandered across the concrete, stepping over the sloping runnels that were channelling the last of the soapy water down to the drain, and inspected the Honda, the Vauxhall, and the Ford. All three had been left by a hire car firm yesterday, for collection by mid-morning. Normally Matt would have been up at six. He would have fully washed, waxed, and valeted at least one before breakfast.

Today he'd done all three, inside and out, by 6.30 a.m. when his father came down to check on him. Since he'd been up and working from 3 a.m. it was no big deal. One hour per car was pretty slow-going. Slacking, really.

His father wandered around the vehicles, checking the dashboards for dust, prodding the seats for too much damp, and running his finger over the hubcaps for missed streaks of road grime. There were none. Matt knew how to valet a car. He'd been doing it since he was ten.

'It's a good job,' Dad said, finally.

Matt risked a shrug. 'Learned from the best.'

His dad ambled over again, put a heavy hand on his shoulder, and peered into his face. 'Why aren't you sleeping?' he asked. 'You need to sleep. Your work will suffer.'

He was talking about schoolwork. It was a small thing, but it meant something to Matt that occasionally—just occasionally—his dad remembered he was still at school. That his whole world did not revolve around sponges, squeegees, and Turtle Wax.

'I dunno,' he said. 'Something keeps waking me up. The last three nights, about half past one. I can't get back to sleep again. This morning I thought I might as well just get up and get some work done and maybe I'll sleep better tonight.'

He didn't say that he'd done the same with a different car the night before ... just the one. But then he'd finished at about 5.30 a.m. and dozed a thin, dreamless almost-sleep on the back seat of the Merc until Dad checked in at the usual time. The slam of the garage door had startled Matt from sleep but, glancing across, Dad assumed he was cleaning the interior. Matt had groggily made scrubbing actions to help that assumption. Then, as soon as Dad had gone, he'd sat back on the spotless leather seat and played a game on his phone until breakfast.

This morning, though, he'd just worked. Three cars. One after the other. Because he was starting to get freaked out and needed to distract himself. Four nights in a row? Waking up at exactly the same time? What the hell was *that* all about?

'Get some proper sleep tonight,' said Dad, giving him a slightly gentler shoulder shake this time. 'And start at the usual time tomorrow. Breakfast now.' He turned and ambled back through the door to the apartment.

By the time they were sitting down to eggs on toast and large mugs of tea, Dad seemed to have forgotten the whole thing. His rages were often like that: a sudden eruption followed by a distracted, forgetful calm. As if nothing was wrong at all.

7

There was nothing to see today, but if there had been a little blood or a fresh bruise or even a black eye, Dad would not have seen it.

Mum would hand Matt a little tube of Savlon or a plaster, so *she* could see it. But she never said anything. Not one word. Except maybe 'He's tired.' Or 'He's stressed.'

If Matt ever responded: 'He's drunk,' or 'He's violent,' Mum would be instantly deaf. She'd been the same with Ben when he used to bear the brunt of Dad's 'tiredness'. Ben, four years older than his little brother Matteus, had long since escaped to the Navy.

The violence was minor. Nothing life-threatening; no big deal. At school he had a reputation for getting into fights, so it was easy to pass the evidence off as a war wound from some scrap with another kid. Anyway, Dad could be OK. When things were going well for him he was generous and cheery —affectionate even.

And Matt didn't think Dad ever hit Mum. That would probably be too much—but she was never bruised or bleeding, although her stuff sometimes got smashed up.

It was all normal. It was all just his life. Nothing much rattled him.

Until now. 1.34 a.m. If he woke up at 1.34 a.m. *again* he might seriously freak out.

The lack of sleep was starting to catch up with him. It hit him late morning in school, during break, as he and Ahmed hung out in the dining hall. Ahmed was going on about some computer game he'd just got into on Xbox, his enthusiastic chatter fading in and out. Matt was opening a bag of Wotsits and wondering whether he had the energy to eat them when the floor abruptly smacked him in the face.

He scrambled to a sitting position, confused, cheesy snacks scattered around him. Ahmed was gaping, and a Year 8 girl with long fair hair was coming across towards him, looking concerned. She crouched down and said, 'Are you all right? You look like—'

Ahmed shouldered her out of the way. 'Mate! You been up gamin' all night?'

The world swam, went a little pink, and then got itself more or less upright and correctly coloured again. Matt gave Ahmed a watery grin. 'Yeah—big time, bro!'

The girl stood, shrugged, and walked away, her school bag slung over her shoulder. She looked familiar. He wanted to say thanks . . . thanks for being concerned . . . but with Ahmed in his face and the girl half a dining hall away by now the moment was gone.

'Seriously—you don't look good, man!' Ahmed was saying.

'Need to throw up, probably,' said Matt, and Ahmed backed away, looking scared. He was a total wimp about anything like that. 'It's OK—I'll see you in Maths,' Matt added, and his friend hared away, relieved he wasn't being called upon for nurse duty.

Matt did not feel sick. Not exactly. But his heart was thudding very fast, and he felt light-headed. He went to the boys' toilets and stuck his wrists under the cold tap, resting his head on the white porcelain soap dimple. The cold water gushed across his skin, cooling his blood, and curled into a spinning vortex above the small plughole. After a couple of minutes the light-headedness passed, and his heart slowed to a normal speed. He stood up and looked at his mirror image in the glass above the basins. His short crop of dark hair was damp on one side, and a smear of cheesy Wotsit dust was on his right ear. The skin beneath his hazel eyes was blueish. It worked well with his puffy red eyelids. His face was pale and peaky. He looked like a zombie.

But worse than all of this was how very, very close he was to bursting into tears.

Matteus Wheeler NEVER cried.

He slapped himself across the face with wet hands, glad there was no other kid in the bogs who could see him. He was NOT going to cry over some lost sleep. He was tougher than that.

Matteus Wheeler NEVER cried.

He kept that in mind for the rest of the day. When Mr Thatcher had a go at him for nodding off in Physics and the rest of the class sniggered. When that girl passed him again in the corridor and gave him a strange look. All through the late afternoon and early evening when he valeted another four cars for Kowski Kar Klean. He kept it in mind as he sank, exhausted, into bed at 10.30 p.m.

And when he awoke at exactly 1.34 a.m., Matteus Wheeler cried.

CHAPTER 3

'Where's the gin, then, Fagin?' Tima pressed her sweaty palms against the tightly laced green bodice and threw a smile across to the boy with a visibly stuck-on beard.

The boy suggested she go easy: too much gin being dangerous for a young girl. It was sound advice from a fellow ten-year-old.

She protested it was the only excitement she got—but that was a lie. Her heart was currently beating so fast she thought it might burst through her costume and land, wet and pulsing, on the stage. Just keeping the words coming out was an incredible effort. But with a school hall packed with kids, parents, and even someone from the local paper, it was an effort she had to make.

Ohgodohgodohgod, some part of her was whimpering as she went into her song. How could she ever have thought that getting the role of Nancy in *Oliver!* was a good thing? How could she ever have believed that she would *enjoy* being up on stage, smothered in sticky make-up, her hair bunched up on her head Victorian style, strutting around, waving her skirt, and singing . . .

'*Life is a game of chance . . .*' The voice was still working—but only just. It was squeezing out of her throat in a thin, reedy whisper. Her fellow performers were glancing at each other, anxiety beginning to show through their acting. What the hell was up with Tima?

A couple of metres above her head, a moth was circling a bright yellow stage light. It was a big, dark, bumbling thing, and it was spiralling closer and closer to her. Tima realized that if she kept singing and leaving her mouth open on the long notes, the moth would probably land on her tongue.

'. . .*if you don't . . . mind . . .*' Finally her voice petered out. That fine strong voice that had won her the part against all the odds—even though she was new at the school, even though the cool girls didn't like her, even though, as a girl with an Arab mum and dad, she didn't have the right colouring—it now deserted her and she finally fell silent.

Mr James, on the piano, went on a few bars while the audience began to shift and murmur uncomfortably, and a few of the kids started giggling nervously. Then he too, petered out, bringing the small school orchestra to a halt with him. He got up from the piano stool.

Tima stood, staring up at the moth, transfixed, her mouth firmly shut. She felt a trickle of sweat run between her shoulder blades, and a sound like taps being turned on at full volume filled her ears, drowning out Lily whining 'Tima—what's the *matter*?!' in some other dimension.

Mr James was on the stage now, announcing an early interval and putting his arm around Tima's shaking shoulders. The audience went into feeble sympathetic applause, and Tima was guided into the wings, seconds before the moth spiralled into the space she'd left.

Everyone rushed in behind her, and Mrs Theroux, the show director, had to tell them all to back off and go to the dressing rooms. 'Lily!' Tima heard her say. 'Change into your Nancy costume; you're doing the second half.' Lily gave a gasp that was both shocked and delighted. Her friends in the chorus whooped.

'Sit down,' said a calm, low voice. Mr James guided Tima on to a small wooden stool in the wings as the curtain rolled across the stage, muffling the sound of the audience making for the refreshments table.

Tima sat.

'What happened?'

Tima didn't answer. Because she didn't know.

'Tima, can you hear me?'

She could hear him. She could see him, too. He had a nice face: curly brown hair and blue eyes. Lily and her friends fancied him, which was just embarrassing. He was ancient—at least 35! But he had been kind to her and worked with her on her singing and told her she was one of the most talented pupils he had met.

'Tima—can you hear me?' he repeated and behind him, Mrs

13

Theroux was asking Ben to go and fetch Miss Lanyard, who was the school first aider.

Eventually she nodded at him and managed to say something. 'Sorry.'

'Are you feeling sick?' he asked. 'Faint? You look a bit pale. You might need to get your head down.'

'I definitely need to get my head down,' she said, and gave a little hysterical laugh. She got her head down every night by 9 p.m. on the dot. And it got itself up again exactly four hours and thirty-four minutes later. And nothing—but *nothing*—she could do would make it get down again until the next night.

Miss Lanyard arrived and made Tima lie on a blanket while she checked her pulse. 'It's very fast,' she said. 'She's got a bit of tachycardia. She feels quite cold and clammy. Where are her parents?'

'They were going to come to see her in tomorrow's show,' said Mrs Theroux. 'I've already phoned them; they're on the way.'

Mum and Dad arrived, full of hugs and comfort, and took her home. By then her pulse was no longer racing, and she just felt as if a very heavy blanket was resting on her. Getting out of the car and walking to her bedroom was like struggling through water.

'You're just overtired, lovely,' said Mum as she tucked her in. She smoothed her hair back off her face. 'Ooh—you've still got a bit of make-up on. Don't worry, though. You can have a nice bath in the morning.'

'It's a school morning,' mumbled Tima, half into her pillow. 'There won't be time.'

'You're not going to school,' said Mum. 'I'm taking you to the doctor. We've got to get to the bottom of all this not sleeping business—although if I'm right and it's just stress about the show, you might sleep through tonight. Now that it's all over.'

Tima felt tears well in her eyes. Yes. It *was* all over, wasn't it? Lily would definitely do the next three shows. She'd got what she wanted after all: the lead role, which she had always felt should be hers, which *would* have been hers if the new girl hadn't shown up, knocking her into understudy position. All Tima's learning of lines, rehearsing of dance steps, practising of songs, and trying to ignore the catty comments from Lily's loyal friends . . . all for nothing. She had embarrassed herself beyond words tonight. It was all over.

'I bet you *will* sleep tonight,' Mum was saying. 'You're nearly asleep now. Off you go—have happy dreams. I will see you in the morning; you'll have a lovely relaxing bath and some toasted crumpets for breakfast, yes? Then we'll go to the doctor and see what she says. Don't worry about a thing. Shhhh. Off to sleep.' Tima felt Mum's kiss on her forehead, and then exhaustion smothered her and she was gone.

Click.

'Oh, you have got to be KIDDING me!' wailed Tima, rolling over and slamming her fist on to her bedside table. Her SpongeBob SquarePants alarm clock shuddered on its little metal feet and ticked on cheerily, marking the seconds. 1.34 a.m. and ten seconds, and twenty seconds, thirty, forty, fifty, 1.35 a.m., ten, twenty, thirty, forty, fifty, 1.36 a.m. . . .

If she didn't stop herself she would just lie like this for hours,

15

watching the clock, mesmerized and fully awake, staring until her eyeballs dried out, experiencing again and again the awful last song on stage like a horror video on a loop.

Tima got up and put her jeans and T-shirt on. She went downstairs in the silence and the darkness. By the dim street light slanting through the window in the front door she found her favourite red jazz shoes and slid them on to her sockless feet. She grabbed her fleecy zip-up top from the pegs above. Her heart was racing again but not in the way it had done on stage. This felt nervy—yes—but more excited nervy than fear nervy. *What are you doing, Tima?* her sensible head was asking. *You can't go out alone in the night!*

Why not? asked her reckless head. *There's nothing out there. Nobody else. I should know; I've been watching this street through the early hours for seven nights now. Nothing ever moves apart from the odd rat round the bins.*

She carefully unlocked the door and eased it open, sliding the key into her jeans pocket. She wouldn't stay out long. She might not even leave the front garden. She just had to do something *different*. Something that might break the pattern of the waking up and the waking up and the waking up and the *THUNK*. The door closed behind her, and she was alone, outside.

The smell of some night-scented plant drifted into her face. It was beautiful, intoxicating. Tima walked across the silvery grass, avoiding crunching along the gravel driveway where Dad's Mercedes was parked. It was a warm night; she unzipped the fleece. A breeze played with her long hair and made the pampas grass on the lawn whisper at her conspiratorially.

She left the garden and walked along the pavement past next door's house. She crossed the road to the small, square residents' green with its white painted wrought-iron bandstand. A moth flew past her. Unlike the moth she'd met on stage, it didn't bother her at all. Other insects danced in the pale light of the street lamps. In a confined space with any of them she would freak out but not out here. Not tonight. They were OK. She was OK.

Her heart had stopped thudding. She sat down on the low brick wall of the green as she realized that for the first time in a week, she was beginning to feel almost normal again. How could that *be* after the night she'd just had? She had no idea. And how could she ever feel relaxed and normal when she was out on her own in the dark? It made no sense.

Maybe this was a dream. Maybe none of this was real at all. The moth went past again, bound for the false moon of a street lamp, and, just to test whether it *was* a dream, Tima held out her hand and, inside her mind, called it to her.

It turned a fluttery arc in the air. It made a course directly for her upturned palm and landed right in it.

She gaped. It tickled as it moved its tiny insect feet and slowly exercised its wings. She could see the fur on its head, the dusting of copper along the brown wing tips, the delicate proboscis that curled out of its face like a party blower.

A dream. Yet . . . that tickle? It must be something she was feeling in her sleep, back in bed. Maybe an insect was *actually* on her hand? She shuddered and flapped the dream-moth away. It was gone in a second, and she was shivering and on her feet and running back to the house.

Come on! Wake up then! Wake up from the dream!

She reached her front garden wall and leapt across it to avoid the noisy gravel (*doesn't matter—it's just a dream*) and then tripped and caught her knee on the brickwork.

The stinging pain and the blood felt pretty real. In the kitchen, the whole business of sticking a plaster on it seemed very undreamlike too.

She made herself some cocoa and took it back upstairs to drink. 2.17 a.m. OK. Apparently this *wasn't* a dream. The moth thing was weird, but maybe there was something on her hand that it had liked the smell of. She hoped she didn't attract any other insect life. She pictured herself running from a swarm of gnats. At her bedroom window, she sipped the drink and chuckled at the nonsense her tired brain kept coming up with. At least it was better than staying in bed and having her negative thoughts going round and round and round in her head.

Outside on the dark sill a chain gang of ants turned a perfect circle and marched on.

CHAPTER 4

His name was Matt. Matteus Wheeler. Elena hadn't had much cause to notice him because he was a year above her in school and—well—she was never going to bump into him in the library or the music room.

He was one of those kids always getting into trouble. Often hanging out with the rougher boys who'd sometimes be swearing and catcalling when she went by. She didn't let it bother her; she wasn't the only one. They picked on a wide range of people. She shrugged it off and didn't respond. They only got worse if you responded. You had to act like you didn't care. And mostly, she didn't.

The trouble with losing sleep, though, was how much it knocked away your ability to cope. She was heading for the music block, a low building of whitewashed breeze blocks and a black tiled roof, when one of them decided to nick her cornet. It was a laugh. Jed Thomason, a tall kid with greasy red hair and a My First Moustache kit applied to his upper lip, swiped the case out of her hands before she knew what was coming.

She gave a yelp of surprise and annoyance and then snapped, 'Give it back!'

'Come and get it!' grinned Jed, holding it high above her reach.

'Oh, you are SO hilarious!' said Elena, but she felt her retort die in her throat. She really didn't have the energy for this. She reached up and jumped towards the small black and silver case and he, of course, held it higher. Then he went to hand it back to her. Then as she sighed and went to take it, he—naturally—threw it across her shoulder to Ahmed Sayid. And Ahmed threw it to Callum Matheson. It could have gone on like this all day. They were falling about with laughter. And why not, thought Elena. Seriously, why bother with *Comedy Live at the Apollo* when you could just stand in a circle and throw a girl's small brass instrument around in its case? Quality entertainment!

Elena came to a halt and stopped watching the show. Her head dropped, and her body seemed to power down. The world went muffled, and the view of her feet was like looking through a gauze: vague and cottony. She let her school bag fall off her shoulder; it was too heavy. She made no fuss. She just went into energy-saving mode, like a neglected laptop. On standby.

The cacophony of teenage boy hilarity went on for another 30 seconds or so, and then she heard a voice say: 'That's enough. Cut it out.' The whooping went on a bit longer, and then the voice came again, louder. 'I said CUT IT OUT.' This was followed by some choice expletives. And then the case was shoved back at her. In confusion she raised her face. Matt Wheeler was standing there. '*Take* it then,' he muttered, and she finally got a grip on the handle and took the weight of it.

She looked up at him, and that's when she knew. His eyes were shadowed and red-rimmed. His skin had a greyish edge to it. There was a faint tremble in the hand that had passed the case.

She knew. She just *knew*. She opened her mouth and whispered: 'One thirty-four a.m.'

He stared at her for a second. And then he blinked, shook his head, and walked away, the rest of the gang trailing, turning their whoops and shouts on him instead. 'OooOOOoooh! Who's got a girlfriend?!' gurgled Jed, like a six-year-old after too many Smarties. As the group turned the corner of the music block, Elena just caught sight of Matt punching him in the chest, sending him sprawling down the grass bank.

A wild giggle escaped her throat as she went in to her class. As she stood in a circle with the other players—two clarinettists and one flute player, all working their way through 'Solveig's Song' from *Peer Gynt*—she felt more giggling building up inside her, shaking and spasming. She kept missing notes while her chest hitched and her shoulders shook.

Finally Mr Gould, the music teacher, snapped: 'Elena, what *is* the matter with you?'

She spluttered through her mouthpiece with a series of uncontrolled squeaks and parps, and everyone turned to stare at her. 'Sorry, sir,' she said, wiping her hair off her face. 'I just . . . got the giggles.'

He told the others to take five and then led her to the side of the room. 'Elena—you're not giggling,' he said, furrowing grey eyebrows. 'You're crying.'

Elena stared at him blankly, only now aware that her cheeks were wet with shed tears. *What the hell?!*

'Do you need to see the school counsellor?' asked Mr Gould, glancing across at the others and clearly feeling out of his depth.

'Erm . . . yes,' said Elena. 'Maybe I do.'

The visit to the school counsellor—a nice lady called Janet—was awkward. Elena tried to explain that she hadn't really been crying, but Janet didn't look convinced.

So she said she'd not been sleeping well. Janet looked very serious, said she should go to the doctor, and signed her off school for the rest of the day.

Feeling slightly bewildered, she left school in the quiet of the mid-afternoon, unaccompanied by 800 other kids for a change. Meandering down the road, her cornet case dangling from one hand, she found herself thinking about Matteus Wheeler. Why had he been nice to her? Why had he stopped the others messing about?

Because he's got it too. Did you see his face? When you said 'One thirty-four a.m.'? Yes. Just for a second, before he'd shut his face down and turned away, she had seen . . . recognition.

He *knew* about 1.34 a.m. She'd suspected it when she saw him collapse in the corridor last week. Now she was certain of it. The realization made goosebumps travel up and down her spine. So now what? She was going to have to talk to him. But how? In school? Not a chance. She frowned, thinking about what she knew of him. She'd heard his parents ran a car valeting business up on the west side of the town. What was it called ... Kowolski? Klowski? His family were Polish, weren't they? Though *he* must be half Polish, with a British surname like Wheeler. So ... maybe she could find out where he lived.

She didn't go home for a nap. For one thing, it wouldn't work—it never did. For another, she needed the internet, and there was no connection at home these days. She turned, instead, down the main road to the public library. If she went now, before other kids came in after school, she should be able to get online without having to wait too long. She was in luck. As she arrived, a middle-aged lady was vacating a seat by a monitor, and she was able to claim a 30-minute slot and get the information she needed.

KOWSKI KAR KLEAN. That was it. A small, single-page website told her where it was and what it could do for her car. Now what? Was she going to go round there right now and meet Matt as he got home from school? What if he brought his mates home with him? Elena shuddered. No way was she risking *that*.

As she remembered the last thing she'd said to him, the answer seemed obvious.

One thirty-four a.m.

CHAPTER 5

The thing about a grazed knee is that you can't explain it away as a dream. Tima knew she really *had* gone out in the night—the evidence of her fall was still there in daylight. And that was fine until she remembered the moth.

Of course, Mum and Dad thought she was just dismayed and humiliated by her terrible performance—and she *was*—but the thing that *really* messed with her mind was that moth. Since when did *moths* come and sit on your hand when you asked? She'd never heard of it.

She even borrowed Mum's laptop and looked it up on the internet, typing in 'Can insects be trained?' and it turned out that some possibly could—but it took a lot of work and equipment and conditioning and anyway, what did she think? That a trained, tame moth had just happened to be passing when she held out her hand?

It was on her mind a lot; she couldn't stop thinking about it. This was another thing she'd noticed about lack of sleep. Insomnia made you weird in lots of ways, and just one of them was obsessing, endlessly, about tiny things. The visit to the doctor distracted her for a while. Dr Jarvis examined her, checking her eyes and ears and chest for breathing issues. They talked about sleep apnoea—a condition that could wake you suddenly in the night.

'You basically stop breathing for a few seconds,' explained the doctor, peering down Tima's throat with her small torch. 'And then the body kick-starts you, and that can make you jolt awake . . . but really . . . I can see no reason why Tima would have it,' she added, glancing over to Tima's mum. 'It's normally overweight adults who get it. The soft tissue at the back of the throat gets fatty and floppy and then causes snoring and breathing problems. It's very rare for a young, skinny thing like you.' She smiled back at Tima. 'You can close your mouth now.'

'My husband said the same,' said Mum. 'He's a surgeon at the Chesterfield,' she explained.

'And Mum's a vet,' said Tima. 'So she could always put me down if it gets too bad.' She gave a slightly hysterical giggle while Mum rolled her eyes.

The doctor laughed and put her torch and stethoscope away. She sat down to talk to them across her desk. 'There are lots of possible reasons for insomnia. Diet, room temperature, disruptive noises in the night, stress, anxiety, dental issues . . . I could go on. But it's not really my field. And as it's been going

2 5

on for a while now, I could refer you to a sleep clinic.'

Mum smiled and nodded.

'But maybe we should wait just a few more days first,' said Dr Jarvis. 'It seems most likely that it's stress—and now that the school show is over, Tima may find her sleep pattern returns to normal.'

Tima stared across the room and out of the window, trying to ignore the drooping feeling inside her as those words—'*the school show is over*'—sank in. She could see butterflies over the lilac tree in the surgery garden. There were six or seven of them . . . she counted three white ones and four reddish ones . . . peacocks or red admirals. They were pretty in a way moths weren't. She still didn't want to pick one up, but they didn't make her feel quite so panicky. After a few seconds she noticed one of them had flown towards the window and landed on it, slowly flexing its delicate brown, red, and blue wings. She wondered if another one would land next to it. A few seconds later, another one—a white one—did. Tima felt a slight fizz somewhere in the base of her spine as she watched the two butterflies, sitting side by side on the glass. *Another one*, she thought. And now another arrived—a peacock. *Another.* A fourth landed. A fifth. And then a sixth—just as soon as she sent out her mental request. They sat in a line, as if awaiting orders. Tima felt the hair on her arms prickle up and her heart pick up pace. Was this *real*? Was she even *here* or still at home in bed, dreaming?

' . . . a few days and see how she is,' Dr Jarvis went on, somewhere distant. 'Get her back to school and . . .'

Tima felt her eyes widening and took a deep breath. She

should stop. She should stop this *now*. But once again she sent out a request. *Form a circle.* And they all did, an instant later, moving across the glass to pick out a circle shape. *What?!* What was going *on*? This was way beyond weird. Way, way beyond a single moth landing on your hand! They were still there—poised as if they were about to do the hokey-cokey. *Put your left wing in, your left wing out—*

STOP IT! yelled a voice in her head.

'Tima? Are you OK, lovely?' Mum touched her face. 'You're a bit sweaty.'

The doctor quickly took her temperature again. 'It's not really elevated,' she said. 'She just needs to sleep and get back her equilibrium. She's sort of . . . jet-lagged.' Behind her, the butterflies had gone back to randomly flitting around the lilac. Tima stopped herself looking again.

'Yeah—I think I could sleep now,' she muttered.

'Are you sure you're OK?' Mum asked, as they went back to the car. 'You seemed a bit rattled in there.'

'It's nothing,' said Tima, pasting on a cheery smile. 'I just . . . had butterflies.'

CHAPTER 6

For the first time 1.34 a.m. was OK. This time she had a *reason* to get up. Elena sprang out of bed as if she'd had a good eight hours.

She dressed quickly in jeans and a sweatshirt and slipped out of her bedroom. Mum was snoring gently as Elena passed by on the landing. She'd taken all her medication after dinner, so she probably wouldn't wake up for hours yet. Her collection of pills totally knocked her out each night. Elena paused and peered through a crack in the door. Mum was lying on her side, eyes closed, mouth open. Her once-pretty face looked puffy and crumpled in the pale moonlight, and her right arm lay outstretched across the edge of the bed, palm tipped open, as if she was pleading with someone in her sleep.

What was going on in her dreams? Elena shook her head

and pulled the door closed. It didn't help to think about it. She had something to do. Downstairs, she pulled on her denim jacket and her trainers—and a pale green beret she'd got for her last birthday. Oddly, wearing a hat made her feel slightly less uneasy about going out alone in the dark—as if wearing a beret could keep any passing mad axemen at bay.

'There's nobody out there,' she murmured to herself as she unlocked the front door and eased it open. It was so quiet around here at night. In some ways, she might feel better if she ever saw or heard the odd bunch of people spilling out from a pub or a delivery driver pulling an all-nighter—but she never did. It was so very empty of humans, this hour.

Apart from that shadowy guy who was taking aim at you, said her inner voice.

Elena pulled the door closed behind her and stepped into the cool night air. The smell was wonderful—heavy with blossom and grass and a sharp, mineral earthiness that she never picked up in the day. The guy taking aim at her wasn't real. She was almost certain he had been a dream. A shadowy figure, lean and wiry, in a billowing long, black coat, with gleaming white hair. Pointing at her. At first, she'd thought, with a gun but later she thought maybe it was just a forefinger with a long, black, blade-like nail on it.

Anyway, a blink later and he'd gone, and she'd been in that stage she reached in the final few hours of sleeplessness—clearly dreaming with her eyes open. Usually around 5.30 or 6 a.m. she seemed to be able to get into bed and drift into something *almost* like sleep. But not actually sleep, because she still heard everything and almost *felt* every second on her clock. And then it would be time to get up and greet the day as if she was a normal person.

No. Weird, dark, finger-pointing guy did not exist. But Matt Wheeler *did* and she wouldn't mind betting that he was awake right now. And maybe he spent time looking out of his bedroom window too . . . and if he did, he might see her. And . . . then what?

She just needed to talk to someone. That was all. Someone else who knew what it was like. Mum didn't understand. She did get a bit concerned whenever she looked closely enough at her daughter to notice the shadows under her eyes—but that didn't happen very often these days. Most of the time Mum was lost inside a cocoon of her own misery—or the drugs that were supposed to be making it better. She probably didn't even remember the talk about going to the doctor that they'd had at teatime.

Elena walked down her road, feeling more relaxed the further she got from home. Even at night. She'd been feeling this way about home for many months now, since way before Dad left. Home wasn't the place it used to be; it was so full of stress and sadness. Her soft-soled trainers made little noise, and as she reached the corner of the road, where it backed on to a small area of overgrown wasteland, she froze, thrilled. Slipping through the dark, a little way along the road in front of her, was her vixen—*Velma*! And it was accompanied by three cubs. They trotted after their mother in the light of a street lamp—all still plump and gorgeous in their brown fluffy baby fur. She caught her breath, not wanting to scare them, and the vixen, scenting her, turned to stare.

Elena expected it to vanish instantly into the dark scrub of the wasteland, but the animal simply stood and looked at her. The cubs trotted on and bumped comically into their mother's tail before also turning to look at the human in their world. Elena felt awash with prickles of delight. She felt a grin split her face. *You lovely thing!* she told the vixen, in her head. *You lovely, lovely thing.*

And still the fox stood there, regarding her from glowing, dark eyes. It seemed completely at ease. Elena crouched down and held out her hand, and, to her amazement, first the cubs and then their mother began to move *towards* her. Wow! How could they be so tame? Mesmerized, she kept still, chuckling with quiet delight as the family came within three metres, two metres . . . one . . . One of the cubs put a nose to her hand. Another one bit one of her trainer laces and tugged at it with a contented squeaky growl.

This was AMAZING.

But most amazing was the vixen. It was now standing close enough for Elena to reach out and touch the fine spray of whiskers on its snout. Elena felt goosebumps wash all over her. 'Do I know you?' she murmured. The vixen leaned in until the warmth of its breath connected them . . . and then touched the cool tip of its nose to Elena's.

Elena gasped.

A second later they were gone. Just as car headlights showed around the corner. Instinctively, Elena leapt into the scrub after them, hiding herself in the dark leaves. But there was no sign of the foxes. No sound, no scent, no movement. When the car had gone, she stepped back out on to the pavement and jumped up and down on the spot a few times, letting out some small gasps and giggles. What a thing! What an *amazing* thing!

She broke into a run and headed for the west side and Kowski Kar Klean. She'd heard of foxes getting quite tame. Probably someone in the neighbourhood was hand-feeding them—that would be it. Even so, what an incredible encounter. She had never felt so . . . *privileged.*

A ten-minute run got her to the car wash place. She found it in darkness. It was an old converted petrol station, built into the hillside next to a steep, winding road. Many years ago there had been fuel pumps under its high, rectangular canopy, but now it was set up with steam-jet cleaners and vacuums on one half of the forecourt, while the other half was boxed in with folding glass doors. This secure bit was where the posher cars were kept overnight. A couple of Vauxhalls and a Ford were parked outside, and a Mercedes and a BMW sat on the concrete floor inside.

What had once been the petrol station shop was now an office area for the valeting business, and above it was a good-sized flat. She guessed this was where Matt lived. But she could see no lights on up there. Or any movement in any window to suggest another bored insomniac was watching her.

Elena began to feel stupid. What had she been thinking? Just because he'd fallen over in school that time and he looked tired yesterday, it didn't mean he was experiencing what she was.

She *thought* she had seen a fleeting reaction when she'd said 'One thirty-four a.m.' to him . . . but it was just as likely she'd imagined it. She imagined a lot of things these days.

She sighed, stepping under the canopy and leaning her forehead against the glass screen. A wave of weariness washed over her, surfed by foolishness. Matt Wheeler was upstairs, fast asleep like a normal person. Truth was, she was the only weird kid on this block.

Then she saw the blue glow inside the BMW. At first it looked like some kind of car alarm light, blinking its security standby pattern. Only . . . it was moving from side to side. Elena pressed her face between cupped palms against the cool glass. Through it she could see the light in the BMW more clearly. It wasn't a car alarm beam—it was the pale blue glow from a phone or a gaming device. It was reflecting off the face of a boy as he punched his thumbs at the gadget, intent and unaware of her presence. Matt Wheeler. In the car. Fully awake.

She watched him for a few more seconds before he finally noticed. His thumbs stopped moving, he raised his face from the game, and he finally locked eyes on her. A few seconds later he was out of the car and pulling the folding glass door open, looking astonished. He stared at her for a long time before speaking.

And when he finally spoke, he said: 'One thirty-four a.m.'

CHAPTER 7

Tima punched SpongeBob SquarePants in the face.

The clock backflipped across the room and landed on the carpet with a metallic yelp of protest, its cartoon hands still pointing to the first hour and the thirty-fourth minute.

'We're so worried about you! I mean . . . it must have been awful. We know this show meant SO much to you.'

Oh *great*. The replay had started IMMEDIATELY. She would lie here for hours now, reliving every last word of that phone call. Eurgh! How she *hated* Lily Fry. *Hated* her!

It had begun with Mum coming into the sitting room last night, just after they'd eaten dinner. She was holding the landline phone. 'Call for you,' she'd said, smiling as if it would be a good thing.

It was Lily—and, Tima soon realized, Clara and Keira too.

The three besties were all huddled around Lily's phone, in Lily's bedroom, getting ready to go and do the next Prince William Preparatory School rendition of *Oliver!*

'We just wanted you to know we were thinking about you,' said Lily, in an 'oh so understanding' voice. 'We're so worried about you! I mean . . . it must have been awful. We know this show meant SO much to you.'

'Oh . . . well . . . thanks,' said Tima, feeling her face get hot. Oh yeah. She *bet* they were thinking about her. She bet they'd been making sure the entire *school* was thinking about her.

'I mean . . . what *happened*?' asked Lily. 'One minute you were OK, and the next—you looked so terrible and your singing was . . . so *weak* and off-key. You must have been SO embarrassed . . .'

She was absolutely loving it. Tima could clearly hear Clara and Keira stifling giggles.

'Well, thanks—but, you know, it's no big deal,' said Tima. 'I've had some problems sleeping. When you don't get enough sleep you kind of . . . lose focus. I'm disappointed, but I'll get over it.'

'Of *course* you will,' said Lily. 'And, Tima, let's face it—this was always going to be a *huge* challenge for you, wasn't it? I mean . . . you've never done a main role before, so you probably didn't really know what it would be like. Nobody blames you for not being up to it.'

Tima gritted her teeth. The phone was sliding in her sweaty hand. 'Well . . . I hope you really enjoy stepping in for me,' she managed at last. 'Have a great time.'

'Oh, I will!' said Lily. 'Last night's show was a-*ma*zing! I got a standing ovation! Keira's mum says a talent agent was there and is thinking about getting me on her books. Can you believe that?'

Frankly, no, thought Tima, but she didn't say it.

'Anyway—we have to go. Last night tonight! And then a party afterwards. Ooh, Tima . . .' her voice dripped with fake sincerity, as if she was talking to a Labrador puppy, ' . . . is there *any chance* you might be able to make it? Everyone wants to see you and make sure you know it's OK to fail sometimes.'

'Thanks, but no,' said Tima. 'Goodbye.' And she hung up and headbutted the sofa.

Now, at 1.36 a.m., the entire conversation had played out once more in her head—but that wouldn't stop it coming around again. And again. And again. There was every chance she would have replayed it 40 times or more before dawn, if she didn't *do* something. Tima got up and went to the window.

The road looked pretty in the starlight, its avenue of trees laden with late spring blossom. They lived in a well-to-do area: all large red-brick Victorian detached houses with sweeping driveways and high gateposts. Her parents were always reminding her how privileged she was, living here, and how fortunate she was to attend a fee-paying independent school. The kids in the local academy would remind her quite often, too, when she walked by in her expensive burgundy blazer, carrying her Prince William Prep satchel and her ridiculous straw hat. They reminded her with very different words, though.

Trouble was, it didn't make any difference how much money Mum and Dad paid; she was still stuck with the likes of Lily,

Clara, and Keira. School wasn't bad, and the teachers were mostly nice. She had a couple of friends—but no best friends. She'd been there less than a year, and most of the best friends had found each other long ago in pre-prep. There were some friendly girls there, but Tima always felt like a bit of an add-on.

Getting the part in the show had been brilliant in many ways—hooking her into an instant community of theatrical kids. But it brought Lily & Co. with it, and they had done all they could to nibble away at her confidence during rehearsals: undermining her performances with 'advice' whenever they got the chance, always disguising it as 'being helpful'.

If she'd been at the school since pre-prep she might even have been friends with Lily, Clara, and Keira. But that was never going to happen now.

'I don't want to be their friend, anyway,' Tima told the night air. The window was fully open, and her voice wafted out into the soft breeze.

Outside looked good.

Really? she asked herself. *After what happened last time? You WANT more freaky insect action?*

No. Not really. But still . . . the road curved away towards the trees, and the bandstand garden and that blossomy scent drifted in to her, tickling her senses and beckoning her like the visible curls of fragrance that lead to the pie on the windowsill in Tom and Jerry cartoons. Outside smelt good. Inside was SpongeBob SquarePants ticking away like a maniac and Lily's sickly sweet malice on an endless loop in her head.

It was time to go.

CHAPTER 8

'I thought it might be a brain tumour.' He said it quietly and gave a little grunt of embarrassment afterwards. 'I was scared,' he added, and Elena stopped in the street and stared at him.

'Matteus Wheeler? *Scared*?!' She immediately wished she'd said nothing because his face clouded and he turned away from her, striding angrily towards the woods. She skipped after him. 'Sorry,' she said. 'I didn't mean to tease. It's just . . . so weird. Until today you were just this boy at school who went around thumping people.'

He stopped and turned to her. 'Is that who I am?' he asked, furrowing his brow. 'Is that what people think?'

She shrugged. 'Well . . . yeah. I mean, you do get into a lot of fights with people, don't you?'

He snorted. 'People get into a lot of fights with *me*,' he said.

'And anyway—you're not the only one in shock. What the hell am *I* doing out in public with a goody two shoes who plays a trumpet and walks around talking like a . . . a . . . children's TV presenter?!'

She snorted indignantly but found the snort turning into a laugh. 'It's a cornet, actually. Not a trumpet. Do you think we maybe have something more *important* to talk about . . . ?' she asked. As soon as he'd said 'One thirty-four a.m.' to her, he'd pulled the folding glass door of the car wash closed behind him and walked swiftly away down the street, clearly expecting her to follow. But they hadn't even started talking about the insomnia yet.

'Not here,' he said, looking around uneasily, as if he really was worried one of his hard-nut mates might see them. 'There.' He pointed through the trees to a clearing that led down to a playground area. By day there'd be local kids hanging out, dangling from the climbing frame and queuing up for the zip wire. Now, of course, it was deserted. Matt made straight for the swings and settled on to one. Elena took the neighbouring swing.

'So . . .' she prompted, after a minute's silence. 'You thought it was a brain tumour?'

He nodded. 'When I fell over that day,' he said. 'You saw me, didn't you?'

She nodded.

'Later on I looked up "losing balance" on the internet.'

Elena sucked in her breath. 'Oh dear.'

'Yeah—a brain tumour can make you suddenly fall over,' he said, twisting the wooden seat around until the metal chains twanged and creaked. 'Or multiple sclerosis. Or . . .'

'A stroke?' suggested Elena. He gave a tight smile. 'I looked
it up too,' she said. 'There are LOADS of other diseases we
might have. Friedreich's ataxia, Wilson's disease . . . *transient
ischaemic attack* is my personal favourite.'

'Yeah . . . right . . .' he said, faintly, as she scooted back and
forth, working the swing into a pendulum.

'But it's not any of those,' she went on, enjoying the night
breeze as it whipped her hair from her face with the forward
swing and wrapped it back around with the backswing. 'It's
something else. Something else is making us wake up at exactly
the same time each night. I mean . . . if it was only me, you
might be able to say it was a brain tumour, or something in my
house waking me up or . . . I don't know what. But *both* of us?
Both of us waking up at one thirty-four? This is something else.'

He twisted the seat right round, 360 degrees, and then let
the anguished metal chains unlock, repel, and spin him jerkily
back in the other direction. 'So . . . do you hear the sound?'

She let her own swing calm to a gentle rock before she
answered. 'I quite like the sound. What do *you* hear?'

He stopped twisting too. 'Like a song . . . kind of. Or like
music really far away.'

She smiled; grateful. It was so good to have someone else
understand. 'Yes,' she said. 'Like a choir or something—but I can
never really make out the tune or the words.'

'Is that what wakes you up?' said Matt.

'I don't know,' she said. 'I can always hear it when I wake and
then it sort of fades away after a few seconds. I can't work out

40

where it's coming from. I thought it was inside my head.'

'Me too,' said Matt. 'I tried to record it on my phone.' He flipped his mobile over and found a sound file on it. 'I set the alarm for five minutes earlier so I could catch it.' He played it back with a shrug. There was a crackly hiss. No song. 'It didn't record,' he said. 'So then I did a search on "hearing things in my head".'

'Oh god!' groaned Elena. 'That must have been fun for you.'

'Yeah. Straight through to the mental health support groups.' He sighed and raised an eyebrow. 'But at least the voices in my head haven't started telling me to kill people. Not yet, anyway.'

'That's good then,' she laughed, surprised that Matt Wheeler made jokes. 'You'll let me know if that changes, yeah?'

Tima walked through the gardens, stopped at the bandstand awhile, and then wandered the streets, her feet quiet in her suede soled jazz shoes. As she walked she felt calmer and calmer. She trailed her fingers along the cool silky leaves of shrubs and bushes in front gardens as she passed. Sometimes insects flew up from them. Moths, gnats, mosquitoes, beetles. Every time it happened she asked the winged creature to fly in an upward spiral pattern. And every time, it did.

She no longer believed she was in a dream. Since the butterfly display team outside the doctor's window, she knew it was real. Or at least it was real to *her*. The only question, really, was whether anyone else could see it. If she were to show anyone, she would find out. If she danced into Mum and Dad's room in the morning and commanded a small squadron of ladybirds to do a Red Arrows fly-past, she would know.

If they saw it, they would freak out. And if they didn't see it, they would take her to a psychiatrist.

Tima didn't know which of these outcomes scared her the most. But right now, here, alone in the night when normally she would have been very edgy and fearful, she actually felt fine. Refreshed and intrigued and exhilarated at what the insect world was willing to do for her.

She felt light on her feet—so light she even did a few dance steps under the blue glow shed by a street lamp. She did a shuffle ball change and even had a go at a triple time step—not easy in jazz shoes. She'd been going to tap and modern jazz dance lessons for two years now and was just beginning to get the hang of it.

She lifted her arms and twirled, and as she did so, two things happened:

1. A rising twist of night flies of all kinds rose above each of her hands, shimmering in the lamplight. She wanted to sing out with delight. Where was her fear? Where had it gone?

2. Her fear came back.

Suddenly, like a guillotine dropping through her soul, fear had her. Because something was under the trees across the road. Something human-shaped but quite un-human in the way it was hanging, shrouded in black, from a low branch. The face was deathly white, and the eyes fixed upon her with a luminous gleam. Tima caught her breath and froze.

The black creature hanging in the tree did not move— except for a slow and deliberate tilt of its pale head, as if it was

42

measuring her up for a sketch . . . or an attack.

Tima's legs abandoned the time step and ran. They went incredibly fast, pounding hard along the pavement. She didn't even know which direction she was going. Every part of her skin was prickling with fear. That thing. That *thing* under the tree! She ran the length of several streets, her tearing, fearful breaths all she could hear; too scared to look back. Then she found herself vaulting a low metal barrier, on concrete supports, which ran the length of the upper end of a recreation ground, and fleeing across the cropped grass. How had she got this far across town so fast? Where were her panicked legs taking her? She should be heading for home!

But she sensed—*knew*—that the dark, hanging shape still lay between her and home. She'd ventured too far beyond the nicely kept Victorian red brick and into the rougher area of pebble-dashed terraces and graffiti-sprayed bus shelters, and now she had no idea how to loop back. She was still new around here.

Turn around! her inner voice yelled. *Look! It's probably not even there now! Look!*

Of course. It was probably nothing more than a shadow and her own imagination.

She looked.

A gurgling scream escaped her throat.

It *was* chasing her, like a billow of black smoke, low above the grass, just a few metres behind her, easily keeping pace, eyes glowing. She could hear it *breathing*. She could hear it *laughing*. That was when she knew she would die.

43

CHAPTER 9

'This is my ninth night.'

Matt was quiet for a while, counting. Then he nodded. 'Me too.'

'I didn't even think much about it until the third night,' said Elena. 'It took three for me to realize what was happening. The time—1.34 a.m. Every time the same. Sleep . . . oh god, I so want sleep. *Real* sleep. Sleep that lasts all night like it used to. I'm only getting about three, maybe four hours. I feel like my mind is disintegrating.'

Matt nodded again. He started to speak, but at that moment they were both silenced by the scream. It was a scream of utter terror, away across the rec by the trees.

They both shot to their feet and then stared at each other.

'Fox,' muttered Elena. 'It'll be a vixen . . . they scream like that, don't they?' But the scream that followed did not sound very vulpine, she thought. It sounded human. And the sob mixed up with it was young and terrified.

Matt started to run towards it. She ran too. Why? She didn't know. The sound was chilling her to the bone, but she knew she could not ignore it. She could make out a small figure stumbling across the grass on the Crabtree Road end of the rec. A girl?

The girl turned beside a clump of trees and seemed to twist in the air. She staggered backwards and fell, shielding her face with her arms, as if she was being chased by something horrific. But Elena couldn't see anything chasing her.

Matt reached the spot before she did. The girl was still shrieking and crying even as he tried to be reassuring. She was slightly built, with long, dark hair, maybe ten or eleven, wearing black leggings and a black jumper and bright red leather shoes. Elena reached them both at speed, skidding on to her knees in the damp grass. She grabbed the girl's trembling shoulder. 'It's OK!' she said. 'It's OK—you're safe.'

The girl finally looked up, her dark round eyes wet with tears and her chin shaking. She drew in a long breath and then turned to look behind her.

'Who was chasing you? Why are you so scared?' asked Elena.

The girl looked around jerkily, her eyes scanning the shadows in every direction. At last they came to rest on Matt and Elena. 'I don't know,' she said, in a small, high voice. 'It was dark and it moved like smoke.'

Elena felt a chill go through her. She squeezed the girl's

shoulder. 'What's your name? What are you doing out here in the middle of the night?'

'I couldn't sleep,' the girl said, with a sniff. She stood up and seemed to shake herself down. She let out a long breath, composing herself, and then said: 'My name's Tima.'

'OK. I'm Elena and he's Matt. We—'

'You can't sleep?' cut in Matt. 'What—just tonight?'

The girl shrugged, still glancing around anxiously. 'Just tonight? No. I haven't slept properly for a week and a half.'

Matt and Elena stared at each other. 'What time do you wake up?' asked Matt, softly.

She glanced at both of them, seeming to understand the importance of the question. 'One thirty-four a.m.,' she said and then blinked as they let out short laughs of amazement. 'What? What about it?'

'Where do you live?' said Elena. 'We'll walk you home and talk on the way.'

Amid the whispering leaves he hung suspended in a downdraught of gloom, watching.

The three of them walked away, strolling through his domain as if they, not he, owned it. He felt his troublesome blood course hotly through his veins. This was not right. This was *his* place. *His time.* If they came here again during his time, there would have to be consequences.

'There must be something that connects us,' said Elena, instinctively lowering her voice as they turned the corner into

Tima's road, well inside what her mum called RichToffsVille. 'Some reason why we're all waking up at the same time. Maybe there are loads of other people waking up too.'

'Maybe,' grunted Matt. 'But if it really *was* loads of people they would all be talking about it by now in the papers and on the radio. My dad has local radio on while we're doing the cars. They talk about *everything* that's going on around here. People phone up to moan about dog poo and litter and the council tax every day. It does my head in—but I haven't heard anything about this.'

'Yes,' said Elena. 'And I've been checking on the Thornleigh web forum. I even asked if anyone was having trouble with noises from the industrial estate waking them up. I thought it might be that, you know? But nobody came back with anything . . . interesting.'

'Adults can't always hear what we can,' said Tima. 'There are some high frequencies that they can't pick up because their hearing isn't so good. I'm ten so my hearing is probably at its peak. Maybe only kids can hear this.'

Elena nodded. 'Good point, littlun.'

'I'm *not* little,' said Tima, looking offended—even though she was only up to Elena's chin.

She seemed very self-possessed for a ten-year-old, Elena thought. She spoke beautifully too, and moved like a dancer.

'Anyway,' Tima went on, 'it doesn't sound industrial. It sounds . . . like a song.'

Again Matt and Elena stared at each other. There was no doubt then. The song. 'Describe it,' said Elena.

47

'It's rich and warm,' said Tima, closing her dark-lashed eyes for a few moments. 'It sounds like it's really far away. Like a stream of music flowing in from another world.'

Elena nodded. 'That's a good description. It is *just* like that.'

Matt said nothing. Elena nudged him. 'Well?'

He rolled his eyes again and shoved his hands deep into his jeans pockets. 'Look—it's just a *sound*,' he muttered. 'And it's waking us up. It's not some mystical thing; it's ruining my life. I fell over in school. Fell *over*. Like a *three*-year-old—in front of my mates. I don't care if you think it's like a night out at the opera; I just want it to stop. We need to find out why it's happening—and make it stop!'

'Do you have any idea what's causing it?' asked Tima.

Elena shrugged. 'I still think it could be a noise or something coming over from the industrial estate. You know— Quarry End. It's not far from my place, and sometimes I hear stuff echoing across from there. It might be that. Maybe they've got a new machine and it starts up automatically at 1.34 a.m. each night.'

'So—let's find out,' said Matt. 'We can go there and check it out tomorrow.'

Elena blinked. 'That's a good idea,' she said.

'Yeah, well, it is *possible* I can have a good idea,' grunted Matt.

'Don't be like that,' she said. 'I know this is weird and freaky—but at least we're not dealing with it on our own now. At least we have each other.'

Tima smiled and nodded. 'It *is* so good to talk about it. And Matt, I know how you feel. You fell over in front of your mates. *I*

48

completely choked in the middle of my solo in the school show. In front of 300 people in the audience. Then a girl I can't stand took over my role. She phoned me up yesterday evening to tell me how great it's all been and how she's getting an agent.'

'Ouch,' said Elena. 'And I cried like a baby in front of my music group today.' She noticed Matt flick her a glance of . . . what? Concern? Guilt? He probably remembered she was on her way to music when his mates started messing with her.

'This is my place,' said Tima. They drew to a halt outside a large Victorian house with a sweeping drive. 'I'd invite you in but . . .' She grinned and looked transformed from the terrified, shivering creature she had been when they'd first found her.

'Yeah—we should probably all be getting back now,' said Elena. 'You never know, we might get an hour or two.' The others gazed back at her, unmoved. They all knew an hour or two was unlikely.

'So—the industrial estate?' asked Matt. 'When are we going to check it out?'

Elena considered. 'It's Saturday tomorrow—well, today, now—so we could go in the daylight. Say we're doing a school project or something—ask some questions.'

'Or we could go at night,' said Matt. 'Do a recce. We're awake anyway . . .'

'Let's do both,' said Tima. 'I have dance classes in Tanwyn Street, and that's only a few minutes' walk away from Quarry End. I go for a couple of hours, starting at ten. Mum drops me off nearby because it's difficult to park, so I can head towards the studio and she won't know that I'm meeting you instead.'

'OK,' said Elena. 'I can meet you there. How about you, Matt?'

He shook his head. 'I'll be cleaning cars for my dad all Saturday morning. You two go on your own. I won't fit in anyway. I don't look right. Nobody will believe I'm doing a school project.'

Elena didn't argue with him. She saw his point. There was nothing school-ish about Matteus. Just wearing the uniform looked like an infringement of his civil rights.

'OK. We'll go in the morning,' she said. 'I mean later *this* morning. And we can all meet up again at 2 a.m. tomorrow. Where?'

'She shouldn't be wandering around on her own,' said Matteus, nodding towards Tima. 'We'll meet here.'

'No way!' said Tima, hotly. 'I'm not a *baby*! And it's not safe for us to meet so close to my house. What if my mum or dad get up for a glass of water and look out through the window while you're hanging around out here?'

Matt gave her a cold smile. 'They'll think I'm checking the house out for a bit of breaking and entering.'

'Well, duh!' said Tima.

Elena laughed out loud and had to clap her hand over her mouth. 'She's right,' she giggled. 'You *do* look like a crim! You can't help it. It's that *face*!'

He scowled at the pavement.

'It's your own fault!' went on Elena. 'You spend all your time trying to look like a gangster. So . . . big surprise . . . people think you're a gangster.'

'I know you're not, though,' said Tima, touching his arm. 'You were really kind to me when I was being chased.'

'Yeah, well,' said Matt. 'Don't you tell anyone.'

'We can meet at the bandstand in the gardens,' said Tima, pointing over to the well-tended grounds of the RichToffsVille estate. 'It's only a short walk for me. I'll be safe. And if anyone tries anything I'll set the moths on them.'

Elena laughed. She liked this little posh girl's sense of humour. It was only when Tima had gone into the house and she and Matt were standing there alone, that she noticed the moths. About twelve of them—brown, black, mottled green, or pale yellow. All lined up on Tima's garden wall like a row of winged sentries.

She shook her head and sighed. 'I really need some sleep.'

CHAPTER 10

'Your names aren't on my list.'

Elena took a deep breath. From the way the young man in the fluorescent jacket was behaving, you'd think they were trying to blag their way backstage at Wembley Arena, rather than across the cracked tarmac of the local industrial estate.

'I know,' she said. 'We haven't made an appointment with anybody. We just wanted to ask some questions for our project. That's all.'

'Ask who?' The young man put down his clipboard, filled with the names of all those blessed people who *did* have a pass to the legendary citadel of Quarry End Industrial Estate.

'Well . . . I don't know . . . people in reception, I suppose,' said Elena.

'It won't take long,' said Tima, waving her own clipboard

and pen. 'We just have to fill in some of the worksheets we got given.'

'Sounds like a weird school project to me,' grunted the young man, picking up his two-way radio and gripping it in both hands, as if it was a lightsaber. There was a *Star Wars* calendar on the wall inside his little white booth beside the road barrier. 'Who wants to send kids around here?'

'It's not for school,' said Elena. 'It's a Duke of Edinburgh's Award scheme thing. We're doing a study on the local industries and what they do for the town.'

The booth Jedi looked unimpressed. 'You still need an appointment.'

'It's a shame,' said Tima, looking downcast. 'I didn't think it would be a problem. Maybe we should phone *The Tribune* and tell them we can't write the story after all.'

Elena glanced at her. What on earth was the girl on about?

'*The Tribune*?' echoed the young man. 'The local paper?'

'Yes,' said Tima. 'We told them about our project and they wanted us to write a story for their youth page.' She sighed. 'I suppose all we'll be able to write about now is how we weren't allowed in. Probably because we're just girls.' She turned away. 'Come on, Ellie. Let's go.'

'Wait!' The young man looked ill at ease now. And well he might, thought Elena. Tima was incredibly convincing. 'You should've said! We've got a publicity person for the park. I'll give her a call.'

He stepped back into his booth and punched out some numbers on the phone. Ten minutes later, Elena and Tima were being shown around Quarry End by a nice lady called Julie.

'It's great to see young girls interested in business and industry,' said Julie, who plumply filled her navy jacket and had curly dark hair and pink cheeks. 'We'll start with Radleigh Insulation Supplies, shall we? Then we'll nip into Castle Ironworks, then Fenchurch Catering Equipment, and then over to Lowland Leather Finishers.'

They set off at a trot along the main access road, which ran the length of what was once a quarry. Five smaller roads branched off at right angles, and assorted metal, brick, and concrete buildings were scattered along them. Some were tall warehouses with trucks and lorries parked outside; others were just single-storey units with a van or two. All were in the shadow of a hill, which, back in the 19th century, had been hacked into by generations of quarry workers and repurposed as a cliff. Its chalky white face was dotted with straggly buddleia bushes and willowherb, clinging to the rough-hewn crags. You could probably climb it, thought Elena; there were plenty of handholds. Who would want to, though? It was three times the height of her house, and if you lost your grip a pile of metal struts or a pallet of breeze blocks would break your fall. She shivered.

There were eleven businesses based at Quarry End, and by the sixth visit, Elena was ready to give up. She had never spent such a tedious Saturday morning. At home, just before she got back into bed around 5 a.m., she had planned a questionnaire for the businesses and neatly drawn it out as a Q&A form, making a copy for Tima. It asked things like 'How many staff work here?'

and 'When did you start out?' Then it went into environmental stuff, like 'How green is your business?' and then, crucially, 'Does your business make noise? Is it running through the night? Have there ever been complaints?'

But what she and Tima hadn't bargained for was how long it would all take. Not because nobody wanted to help, but because nearly everybody really DID want to help. Way too much. The people they spoke to went on for *ages*. They must be really, really bored with their work and seeking a distraction, Elena thought, trying to look fascinated. Or just very kind. After all, Tima looked quite cute.

An hour later they had spoken to eight of the businesses. Two of them did not operate on a Saturday, so there was nobody there to ask. There was one more left. And what had they learned? Nothing helpful at all. Nobody had any idea what happened at night because none of them were ever there. They all went home and slept like normal people.

'Remind me whose idea this was?' muttered Tima as they followed Julie across to Sentry SuperSacks. A huge packaging warehouse tucked right against the quarry cliff face, its massive doors were rolled open wide to reveal floor-to-ceiling shelving filled with packing boxes, envelopes, paper, and bubble wrap.

'Mind out,' said a burly man in a boiler suit as they reached the threshold. 'Coming through with the dead!' He was carrying a cardboard box full of feathers.

No. Not just feathers. It was birds. A pigeon, a rook, and two starlings. All dead.

Elena and Tima stopped in their tracks.

'More?' said Julie. 'Oh, that's a shame, isn't it? I wonder why they keep coming in?'

'Search me,' said the man, shrugging. 'Stupid things. They fly in—and not one of them can find their way out again. First thing in the morning—dead on the floor—right up the back. You'd think they'd fly out to the light, wouldn't you? Even at night, there's lamplight! Daft beggars.'

'Um . . . is that normal?' asked Tima.

Julie shook her head. 'Not really. I mean, every so often a bird will get into a warehouse and flap around being annoying and leaving droppings all over the stock. But they usually find their own way out. This dozy lot,' she waved at the box with disdain, 'don't seem to have a birdbrain in their heads.'

'How long has it been happening?' asked Elena, trying to peer into the box.

The man hefted it up on one shoulder and pursed his lips in thought. 'A couple of weeks,' he said. 'Shame I don't like rook and pigeon pie!' And he went off to dispose of the bodies in a tall metal bin in the car park.

'Wait,' called Elena. She ran across to him with her clipboard and cut to the most important question. 'Have you noticed anything else odd going on? Maybe . . . a strange noise or something? Maybe . . . at night?'

He looked at her curiously. She held up the clipboard, plastering on a smile. 'For a . . . survey. A project we're doing . . . ?'

He furrowed his brow under greying hair. 'Sounds? At night? Well, I'm not here past seven or eight at night, so I wouldn't know, love. No, nothing—just dead birds. With scary dead eyes . . . wooOOoooh!' He flapped his hands at her in what he probably thought was a spooky way. 'Weird enough for you?' he chuckled. 'That's probably the last of them,' he added, glancing at the bin.

Then he went on his way. Tima didn't say anything to her, but they both knew it was time to go. Elena thanked Julie warmly. 'We've taken up a lot of your time—it's very kind of you.'

'Not at all,' said Julie. 'You saved me from a morning of admin. It's been a nice change, spending time with some bright young things like you. I hope you write a nice piece for the paper.'

'Oh, we will,' said Tima, glancing guiltily at Elena.

They waved goodbye to the young man in the booth as they left, and he waved back cheerily.

'I feel bad,' said Tima.

'I know,' said Elena. 'Maybe we *should* write an article for *The Tribune*.'

'Not about *that*. About the birds. About that warehouse. Didn't you feel it? It was . . . not good.'

'The dead birds were creepy,' admitted Elena. 'But otherwise it looked quite normal.'

'Not normal,' said Tima. 'It was empty.'

'Empty? It was *stuffed* with bubble wrap and envelopes! It was packed with packaging!'

Tima slowed down and looked at her feet. She spoke quietly. So quietly that Elena thought, at first, she'd misheard.

'There were no insects.'

Elena paused, weighing up the best response. 'I think you're a bit overtired,' she said, eventually. 'This insomnia . . . it messes you up. You probably need some food too.'

'No spiders either.'

Elena felt herself get impatient. It was something that happened more and more easily these days. Insomniacs didn't have much patience. 'What are you *talking* about? How on earth could you know that? Of *course* there were spiders. Thousands of them! It's a great big dusty warehouse.'

Tima fell silent. 'I want to go home now,' she said, suddenly sounding very young. 'I've got to get back to meet Mum. I'll see you tonight at the bandstand.' And she scurried off without a further word.

Elena stood on the corner and watched her go. She felt a chill. Tima seemed normal enough, but first there was the 'dark shadow' chasing her, which neither she nor Matt had seen any evidence of—and now she was muttering about missing insects. Perhaps the girl was a little bit messed up in the head.

Then another thought occurred to her. Perhaps *she* was a little bit messed up in the head too . . .

CHAPTER 11

Matt only realized he'd fallen asleep when his head started to slide down the windscreen. His mouth caught on the clean glass like a rubber squeegee as his slumbering face stuttered and puckered with confusion. Had anyone been inside the car it might have looked like some kind of human-jellyfish mutant attack. A slow, confused attack.

He had been struggling all morning, and now, at nearly lunchtime, he was barely able to keep his eyes open.

Last night had been great in many ways—the relief of finally sharing his problems with two other people who completely understood; realizing he wasn't just some lone freak in this town; the idea of some kind of plan. Checking out the industrial estate wasn't much, but it was a start. But the excitement had made it even harder to switch off and get a little doze in when he finally got back into bed at dawn. On Saturdays he didn't have to get up so early; his car wash duties normally started between 9 and 10 a.m., depending on how many customers were waiting. On quiet days, Dad would let him knock off around lunchtime and have an afternoon off.

He had managed maybe an hour of sleep to add to the three hours he'd got before 1.34 a.m. In total, four hours, tops. After breakfast he worked on the cars on some kind of autopilot, dead on his feet. Dad had clouted him on the back of the head twice by mid-morning, for missing bits of wax and forgetting to do an ashtray. Now his son had just topped it all off by crashing out and dribbling all the way down the windscreen of a classic Jaguar.

'What's wrong with you?!' Dad hauled him upright by the back of his T-shirt and shook him. Above him a startled bird—a starling—flapped away from its roost on the Kowski Kar Klean sign. 'Have you been up all night on your PlayBox? I told your mother she should never have bought that for you. It's turning you into a mindless zombie. What use are you to me like this?'

Matt was too tired even to smirk at his father's total lack of gaming savvy. *PlayBox*?! 'I told you, Dad,' he said. 'I can't sleep. I don't know why.'

'I know why!' snarled Dad, and Matt noticed, not for the first time, the whisky on his breath well before lunch. If he'd been more awake he might have run. 'You waste time on your games and your phone and you don't think THIS is important, so you sleepwalk through it! Well, enough's enough. ALEKS! ALEKS!'

His wife was out on the wet concrete in seconds, wearing that half-smile she always pasted on when she wasn't yet sure how far gone he was; hoping to distract him or mollify him before he blew. Sometimes it even worked, but not today.

Dad shook him again, pinching hard into his T-shirt. 'Bring down his PlayBox!'

This time Matt was too tired *not* to laugh. He couldn't hold it in; a hysterical giggle slid out of his throat before he could stop it. His father slammed him against the side of the Jag. 'You think this is FUNNY?'

Matt shook his head feebly. Above him three starlings flew in a circle and roosted on the edge of the car wash canopy. In his delirious state he thought he heard one of them echo back, 'FUNNY? FUNNY?' Now Mum was back, carrying his Xbox, letting the plug and controller skip and bounce across the ground on the end of their flexes. Her face was full of dread now. 'Here it is,' she mumbled, looking around to see where she should set it down, but Dad swiped it out of her arms and flung it down beside the jet spray. He deluged it in foam and then snatched up the pressure hose and beat the console sideways across the ground with the force of the water. Mum stood back, arms folded, trying not to look as aghast as she felt. It had been Matt's birthday present only three months ago. Now it was very, very clean. And ruined.

Dad finally finished the jet-spraying and then kicked the whole thing under a mud-spattered Vauxhall estate. It slid and jerked, the plug and controller both spasming on the end of their flexes, before vanishing under the exhaust.

Then he turned to Matt and held out his hand. 'Phone,' he said. 'Now.'

Matt handed over the small mobile. It was no great loss, he told himself. It was a rubbish phone anyway. But it *was* a great loss. He could already feel his world spinning apart without it. None of his mates would be able to contact him now. He would have no idea where they were or what was going on. When he finished work he would not be able to find them. Even if Dad let him use the landline, he couldn't remember their numbers. He'd never needed to; they were all stored in his phone's memory.

'Now—go to your room,' said Dad. The violence seemed to have left his voice; now it was just filled with disgust. 'You go in and go to bed and do not come out again until six o'clock. Make up your sleep.'

He staggered back up the stairs to the flat, a strange heaving motion going on in his chest. Mum hurried after him. As he reached his bedroom door she said: 'Matt—he'll feel bad about it later. He doesn't mean to hurt you.'

Matt spun around and stared at her. 'Yes he does!' he hissed. 'He always does!'

His mother dropped her eyes to the hallway carpet and shrugged her thin shoulders. 'He's just been under a lot of stress lately,' she murmured, flicking a lank strand of hair off her face.

'He's been under a lot of stress *my whole life*!' gulped Matt, wiping some wetness from his cheek. From the jet spray, probably. 'Have you ever known him when he *wasn't* under stress? And drinking too much? And taking it out on me and you? And Ben? But Ben got away,' he muttered, bitterly. 'I'm still stuck here.'

'He—he doesn't mean it,' his mother insisted, her face crumpling.

'Well, I wonder what will happen the day he DOES mean it!' Matt turned away from her and went into his room, slamming the door. A wave of misery hit him. And guilt, because it wasn't her fault, was it? It was Dad. Always Dad. He went to his window and peered down at the car wash below. His father was continuing to work on a Mitsubishi 4x4, polishing its dark red bonnet to a fine gleam that reflected the sky and one or two birds flitting across it. The man's face was set like a mask.

Matt couldn't see the Xbox. It must still be under the Vauxhall. The thought of it gave him a physical pain in his stomach. He stared at the back of his father's head and wished he was bigger and stronger, so he could fight back. One day he would be. That day could not come soon enough.

A black shadow suddenly landed on the windowsill outside, making him jump. It was one of the starlings. A sleek, dark bird with shifting oily rainbow patterns on its wings, the starling sat right there, inches away from him on the other side of the glass. It must know he was there. He tapped on the pane, and the bird turned and looked at him. Just . . . looked. Matt stared back into its bead-like eyes, baffled. Why wasn't it flapping away in fright? Instead it manoeuvred itself around on the concrete sill as if it wanted to get a better look at him. Matt stared back at it. And then shook his head. The bird shook its head too. And then flew up past the window and out of sight.

Blinking, Matt let his gaze drop once more on the loathed figure of his father, who was flicking a chamois leather one last time across the Mitsubishi's bonnet and standing back, arms folded, admiring his work.

There was a sudden rush of dark shapes dropping past his window. They swooped and twisted in the air like a Red Arrows formation. He just had time to notice his father glance up before multiple white spatters appeared on the bonnet. Dad let out a shout of rage and twirled around, glaring up.

Matt gave a hoot of delight and clapped his hands to his mouth.

Then the starlings turned and strafed the roof of the car a second time, coating it with sticky white and grey droppings that splashed on impact, sending star shapes out in all directions. It was quite artistic. But Dad was howling with rage now. His arms were pistoning upwards as if he was trying to punch the birds away.

He didn't notice his son in the upstairs window, hopping from foot to foot and screaming with laughter, tears running down his cheeks. Matt could not believe what he'd just seen. Then he realized the starlings were moving again—in a weird, fluctuating flock above the houses just across the street. How many were there now? There had been only a dozen or so before, and now . . . a hundred? Two hundred? Three?

Suddenly they struck out like one entity, encircling the car and his father, who was now staring, open-mouthed, at this winged visitation. The birds flew faster and faster, blurring into a screeching airborne carousel. Matt held his breath, his eyes stretching wide with amazement. Then—as one—*every single starling* deposited what must have been the entire contents of its birdy bowels all over the car and the man raging next to it.

Matt gave one more shocked, hacking laugh and then

dropped to his knees, stunned. The starling swarm scattered to the heavens and seconds later all that could be seen was one dripping 4x4 and one car wash owner, wiping bird poo off his face, blinking as if he was in a dream.

And one last bird, flying one last loop and crying out something that sounded eerily like '*FUNNY?*'

CHAPTER 12

Tima lay in the grass. Very still. Their gardener was due to come and mow it all tomorrow, but right now it was high and lush and full of life. A couple of weeks ago Tima would never have lain *in* the grass. She would have put down a blanket or a beach mat and anxiously flicked off any insect that wandered on to it.

Now, though, she felt quite content as the cool green blades tickled her ears and the backs of her knees. Ants, spiders, beetles, centipedes, grasshoppers . . . they were teeming around her, but, politely, they didn't wander *across* her as she gazed at the blue sky through half-closed lids. She wasn't asleep, but she was *almost* dozing. Half dreaming. At one point she thought she saw a flock of birds twist and turn in the sky and form strange shapes in the air: spirals, orbs, lines . . . One of them was calling out, cracked and crow-like: 'FUNNY! FUNNY! FUNNY!' And it definitely *was* funny—but as soon as she got up on her elbows, blearily staring up into the sky, the birds dropped into a random flock and flew away.

It was the insomnia, of course, sending her mind doolally. She was still freaked out from the trip to Quarry End. It had been nice to spend time with Elena. Even though she was three years older, Elena didn't talk down to her or boss her around. Meeting Elena—and Matt—was the only thing that was stopping the panic inside her from spiralling out of control.

But the thing at the warehouse this morning. What had she told her new friend?

'There were no insects.'

'No spiders either.'

Like Elena had said, how could she *know* that?

She had no idea how she knew—she just knew. Seriously, though, how *could* any human being look at a huge warehouse and know, without question, that not a single non-human creature was alive in it, from a rat to a flea? Beneath the sounds of the handful of humans in the area, the whole place had been silent as a grave.

OK, Tima. Be logical, she instructed herself. *You saw the man carrying out the bird corpses and that just set up a funny idea in your head. You dreamed up this weird idea and then you thought it. And then you did the really dumb thing and SAID it. Out loud.*

That was probably it. Only . . . she hadn't *thought* what she'd said to Elena. She had *felt* it.

'You're just overtired,' she mumbled to herself, as the clouds drifted over her. 'That's all.' She would say that when they met tonight. She didn't want Elena and Matt to think she was loopy.

Mum wandered down the garden with a pair of secateurs, heading for the far end where she wanted to prune something. 'All right, sleepy girl?' she asked as she passed. Tima smiled and nodded. 'Just soaking up some sun,' she murmured, and Mum smiled and disappeared down past the summer house.

Tima rolled on to her side. She could see a grasshopper in a tall clump of weeds. It was almost the same shade as the stem it was clinging to, flexing its hind legs across its wings and sending out high-pitched chirrups. Tima stretched out her arm, laying it, palm up, along the grass. *Hello*, she sent, from her mind. The grasshopper stopped chirruping. *Hello*, she sent, again. It turned towards her on the stem, and then, in the blink of an eye, it was on her palm.

She pulled in a short breath and then sat up to gaze at it in wonder. 'You came to me,' she murmured. 'Like the moth . . . like the butterflies. Do you really understand me?' The grasshopper worked its legs again, sending out another chirrup. 'You're beautiful,' she told it. Because it was. She had never thought such a thing before. She'd never looked closely, of course. If a grasshopper had landed on her two weeks ago, she would have shrieked and flicked it away. She had never *looked*. Now, she held it close to her face and studied it, fascinated. The creature was built solidly, its body in fluidly moving parts that might have been made from green aluminium. Its abdomen was decorated with stripy black markings, between powerful slingshot legs in shades of apple—pink and green. Its face was long and almost horse-like, with dark-brown, oval eyes below short, pointed feelers.

'Where are your friends?' she asked it, sitting up slowly. 'Can I meet them?'

At once there was a patter across her arms and legs and around a dozen grasshoppers were resting on her, their feelers waving curiously. She caught her breath and then laughed in delight. 'Wow! Hello! Hello, everyone!'

Now that she had their attention she wasn't quite sure what to do with it. More were arriving now, spattering across her like big drops of green rain. 'You're all just . . . lovely,' she said. 'Can you *really* understand me?' Their feelers waved, but that could have been for any reason. 'If you understand me,' she said, 'please turn around in a circle.'

And they *did*. They all did: rotating on the spot, feelers waving. 'Thank you! Oh, thank you!' she breathed, delighted laughter spilling out of her throat.

'Tima, who are you talking to?'

Her mother's voice was like a bucket of cold water on her head. She spun around in shock, and the grasshoppers pinged back into the grass in a firework display that lasted less than a second.

Mum stood behind her, secateurs and a bunch of droopy snipped-off blooms in her hands. She looked bemused.

'Nobody,' said Tima. Her voice sounded shrill and guilty, as if she'd been doing something wrong.

'Nobody?' Mum knelt down next to her and smoothed some hair off her forehead.

'Well . . .' Tima thought feverishly. What could she say to make this seem . . . normal? 'I was, kind of talking to the grasshoppers.' She giggled. 'You know . . . because grasshoppers are SO up with all the garden gossip.'

'Oh?' Mum raised a dark eyebrow. 'And what's the latest?'

'Nothing much,' said Tima, shrugging. 'The ants are probably where it's at.'

'You do know you were talking out loud to them, don't you?' asked Mum, that eyebrow still up.

'Yeah, well . . .' Tima shrugged.

Mum stroked her hair and smiled thinly. 'Darling, don't be upset, but I have to ask you this . . . Are you actually *hearing* them talk back to you?'

Tima gave a dry cackle. 'Of course not. They're *grasshoppers.*'

Mum sighed. 'Phew,' she said, and went back into the house.

Tima chuckled to herself, still fizzing inside. She could *talk to insects*! Just . . . *wow*! But she'd better be careful. She'd given Mum and Dad quite enough to worry about recently without now convincing them she was barking mad. It was true that the grasshoppers weren't *talking* to her, as such, but they had definitely been communicating. They had been doing exactly what she asked them to. Now probably wasn't the time to share this with Mum and Dad, though. Tima felt another fizz of excitement. She couldn't wait to tell Elena and Matt about all this.

There were bees in the lavender that grew along the border near the garden seat. She could hear them buzzing as they busily collected pollen from the tiny purple flowers. Tima got up, walked across, and settled herself on the bench, next to the lavender. She rested her hand on the sun-warmed wooden

70

armrest and sent a message to the bees. *Come to me.*

Her heart thrummed with excitement and nerves. Grasshoppers and moths were one thing, but these were *stinging* insects. She was taking a risk here. A bee landed on the back of her hand, feelers waving. She took in a quick breath. *Hello.* Another followed. And then several, landing along her arm, gently tickling. *Turn towards me,* she sent. Around a dozen honeybees turned to face her, feelers waving, delicate filmy wings folding back.

Of course, it wasn't unheard of. She'd seen a documentary once where a beekeeper had stood quite still and grown a bee *beard.* He'd captured the queen and attached her, in a little cage, to his chin so her entire colony swarmed on to his chin and hung off it like an actual beard. Afterwards he hadn't been stung even once.

As this thought flitted through her mind a bee landed on her left cheek. She jumped and twitched but didn't swipe it away. *Really?* she asked. *Can we do this?* Another one landed on her chin. Another on her ear. *Not there—too buzzy, too loud.* It obediently moved down to her jaw. The bees felt tickly on her skin—but very gentle. More came. *Many* came. She kept her mouth shut and asked one or two of them, *politely,* not to go up her nostrils. They, *politely,* retreated. None of them approached her ears again, or her eyes, but they swiftly colonized her neck and shoulders.

Tima's whole body was thrumming now. It was the most extraordinary sensation—a little like being in a gentle electrical current, with the constant soft movement of thousands of tiny feet across her skin. Bees now clustered along both arms, dripping from her wrists like silken sleeves. Two ovals were forming on her bare knees, a twinkling mass of wings, feelers, and furry, pollen-dusted bodies. She should have been freaking out, but all she felt was an intense calm and something else she could only call *joy*. Her smile lifted the bees on her face in a kind of Mexican wave as she got ready to wish them well and send them back.

Then she heard her mother scream.

CHAPTER 13

Three of them. The same as last night. So they'd found each other then. How sweet.

He swayed gently beneath the dark whisper of a beech tree, pondering. This was invasion. There was no doubt about it—and if he let it go the invasion could get worse. The bandstand was one of his favourite haunts, and now they'd just stamped into it and taken occupation.

This part of town, at night, was *his*. He could tolerate shift workers passing through. They were dull: focused on heading to work or their homes. They never ventured off the roads and pavements, so he mostly let them be. Drunken partygoers were also tolerable. Better than tolerable, in fact. These were his entertainment. They were perfect targets for his kind of fun. He could play with them, take what he needed from them, get maximum effect—and nobody would ever believe them in the morning.

Possibly even better were those out on criminal business, planning to thieve or rob or attack. He really, *really* enjoyed those. The looks of amazement on their faces when they realized what was happening, too late, too fast. The sting of it! The thrill, when they realized *what* he was. The way their eyes widened and then screwed shut as their *whole world order* changed in just a few seconds.

Yes. Yes, he really DID exist.

But these three were different. For one thing, they were too young. All of them, even the boy—way too young to be out in his world. The smaller girl? Stupidly young to be out. The chase he'd given her last night should have convinced her of that, and yet, here she was again, cool as you like. Well, she had two friends now, didn't she? What was stopping them meeting up in the daytime, though, like every other normal kid?

He watched for a long time, weighing up the options, thinking about their fast-flowing blood, feeling a bitter pulse inside. Taking their day and *his* night; this was greed.

He could just scare them, of course. He had no doubt that he could run them out of his territory in a matter of seconds, never to return. But where was the fun in *that?* As much as he felt the urge to chase them off, the need to find out *why* they were here was stronger. Some study was required. Once he knew more, he could decide their fate.

He rose into the branches, stilled himself utterly, and listened.

CHAPTER 14

Tima looked like a cat burglar. Elena grinned as her new friend sat on the steps of the bandstand and double-knotted the laces on her black leather jazz shoes. She was wearing skinny black jeans and a black long-sleeved T-shirt, and her hair was hanging in a single dark plait down her back.

'You really know how to dress the part, don't you?' said Elena. She herself was just wearing trainers, jeans, a green zip-up top, and the green beret. And a small backpack with a couple of torches, a bottle of water, and her mobile in it, among other useful things.

Tima smiled. 'I like costume,' she said. 'And I like to wear things I can run in. You never know when you might need to.' She glanced across the white-painted wooden balustrade of the hexagonal bandstand, towards the dark trees that hemmed the park. Elena followed her gaze and for a moment thought she saw something pale, glowing in the branches. As soon as she'd blinked, though, it was gone.

'You worried that shadowy thing might come after you again?' she asked.

Tima shrugged.

'Are you sure it wasn't . . . I don't know . . . a black cat or something?'

Tima gave her a *look*. 'Yeah, sure,' she said, stonily. 'It was a *cat*.'

Matt said nothing. He just stood with his hands deep in his jeans pockets and glanced around the night sky. He didn't speak at all as they related the events of their morning at Quarry End—until they got to the dead birds bit. Then his face lifted immediately, and he narrowed his eyes at them both. 'Dead birds? What kind?'

'Pigeon . . . rook . . . starling, maybe,' said Elena. 'Does it matter?' He stared at her for a few seconds, then shook his head and sank into himself again.

'Come on, Matt,' said Elena. 'We need to go back there now. See what we can find out with nobody else around. That was your idea . . . remember?'

They trooped out of the bandstand and headed across town towards Quarry End.

'Matt, are you OK?' Elena asked, as they fell into step. She kept her voice low, aware of the way it resounded among the hard pavements and brick houses.

'I don't know,' he said, surprising her. 'Weird stuff keeps happening.'

'You're telling *me*,' muttered Tima.

They walked on for a few moments, and then Elena prodded, 'Well? Are you going to tell us?'

'You'll think I'm making it up,' he said.

It was Tima who voiced exactly what Elena was thinking.

'Matt! We're all in this together. You have to tell us stuff. It could be important.'

She sounded way older than ten, thought Elena.

Matt walked on for a few more seconds, and then he said: 'These birds ... starlings ... they did something really weird at the car wash today. They ... kind of ... did want I wanted them to do.'

Tima stopped and grabbed his arm. 'What?! What did they do?' Her eyes were huge in her head.

'Well,' went on Matt, glancing around to be sure they were still alone. 'My dad had a go at me because I fell asleep on a windscreen. He thinks I've been staying up all night on my Xbox. So ... he got Mum to bring it down and then he soaked it with the power jet. Just ... drowned it.'

Elena heard herself groan. Matt's voice was steady, but she knew what gaming meant to most boys in her year. That must have *hurt*.

'Then he took my phone off me,' went on Matt, as if this, too, was nothing much. 'And sent me up to my room. And while I was watching him at the window, this bird showed up ...'

By the time he'd finished his story, Elena and Tima were both convulsed with laughter. Matt grinned a bit too, for the first time that night. He ran his hands through his hair and shook his head, laughing, and the weight on him seemed to lift. And then, as one, all three of them sobered up and let out long breaths. *Weird* did not cover it.

'So . . . you think the birds kind of read your mind?' said Elena.

'Yeah,' said Matt. 'I just . . . *hated* him. I *wanted* him to be as upset as he made me.'

'Well, I think you scored there,' said Elena. 'Any chance your Xbox made it?'

'Mum got it back and tried to dry it off after tea,' he said. 'It's not working, but she's put it in the airing cupboard. She thinks the warm air might do the trick.' He didn't look convinced.

'And the phone?' asked Tima.

'Nope.'

'Well, your day was pretty freaky,' said Tima. 'But wait until you hear about *mine*.' She glanced at them both and grinned. 'Not here, though. I want to tell you, but I think the best thing is to show you. I'll show you when we get to Quarry End.'

'Just *tell* us!' muttered Matt.

But Tima wouldn't.

'You are *so* theatrical,' laughed Elena, giving the smaller girl's dark plait a tug.

Tima lifted her hands and did a few elegant dance steps as they walked. 'It's true,' she said.

They moved on through the silent streets, past the dark loom of Thornleigh Town Hall and along the flat concrete road towards the industrial estate. They passed the shadowy bulk of the town's gas power station on the way, its lone, low aircraft warning light hanging up high above them on the metal stack, like a red star.

There was a gentle hum from the power station, and lights shone at the far end of the building. The trio slunk past it, and Elena, with a sudden realization, whispered: 'We should probably check the power plant out as well . . . *that* place could be making a noise at 1.34 a.m. to wake us up too.'

'If we don't find anything at Quarry End,' whispered back Matt, 'you and Tima can go and do your Duke of Edinburgh project there too.'

'It's not there,' murmured Tima.

'How do you know?' muttered Matt.

'I just do,' she said.

Five minutes on, they reached the mismatched, boxy buildings of Quarry End, picked out starkly in the orange veil of light cast down from lamps on tall metal poles. A metal mesh fence ran around the perimeter with threatening spikes along the top. The sturdy iron gates to the estate were firmly closed and padlocked. Next to them, the booth where the unhelpful security guy had been stationed was empty and dark. Booth Jedi obviously clocked off at teatime.

'I didn't think it would all be locked up,' said Elena, stopping abruptly. 'That kind of messes up our plan.'

Matt snorted. '*That*,' he said, 'is not locked up. Anyone could get in there.' He walked across to a recycling bin—a large metal skip on wheels with a hinged blue lid lying flat on top. It was big enough for all three of them to climb into. Or on to. Matt gave it a hard shove, and it moved with a hollow rumble. He grinned, shoved again, and then stared at them. 'Well, come *on!*'

Elena and Tima joined him, and their combined effort drove the skip bumpily across a grassy strip. They shoved it close against the security booth. It reached two-thirds of the way up.

'Give me a bunk-up,' said Matt.

Elena looked around. There were signs warning of 24-hour CCTV surveillance and dog patrols. 'What if we're being watched on camera?' she hissed.

Matt snorted again. 'Can you see any cameras?' They all looked and all concluded that no, they couldn't see any.

'But what if they come round with a dog patrol?' added Elena.

'It's just a *sign*,' said Matt, as if she was an idiot. 'They can't afford a proper security system here. It's a cheap, low-rent park. A padlock and some scary signs are about all you get out here. The buildings inside might have better security, though. But we won't know until we look. Come on—help me up!'

Elena laced her fingers together and put her hands into a hammock for him to use as a step. Tima came over and added her own hands to make it stronger. Matt leaned on Elena's shoulder and stepped on to their meshed fingers. A heavy jolt and he was up on the top of the bin. He grinned down at them and held out one hand. 'Tima first.' Elena boosted Tima up easily, and then the pair of them leant down and helped her scrabble inelegantly up the side of the bin. Once all three were on it the lid started to buckle, so Matt climbed quickly up on to the roof of the booth. It was only a three-metre drop to the ground on the other side, and he managed it easily. He stood beneath them and advised: 'Don't jump from the top—get on your belly and slide your legs down over the edge, hang down and then drop. I'll catch you.'

It wasn't very graceful, but Elena did what he said. Tima followed, moving lithely like a black cat.

They stood in the shadow of the booth for a few moments, catching their breath and taking stock. Elena felt a thrill course through her. Matt was right about her being a goody two shoes. She had never really broken any rules before—and although she wasn't planning to slide into a life of crime, there was something exciting about breaking some boundaries. Literally, in this case.

'OK,' she whispered, 'the warehouse we want is right at the far end of the estate. Should we just casually walk over to it or should we creep around the perimeter in the shadows?'

'I say we creep,' said Tima, her eyes shining.

'We might set off security lighting in the darker areas,' said Matt. 'I say we just swagger down the road like we own the place. It's the furthest point from any cameras on the buildings.'

Elena pulled her beret down over her forehead and tucked her chin down. Matt pulled up the hood on his zip-up top. Tima just walked on without attempting to look inconspicuous at all. 'If you spot a camera,' she said, 'just tell me.' There was a confidence in her voice that made Elena envious. She wished *she* had been that together when she was ten. She guessed it was the effect of going to a posh, independent school. All the kids from Prince William Prep seemed very confident.

The first couple of buildings were in shadow. No security

lighting suddenly flared out from them. Maybe Matt was right and you had to get a lot closer to trigger it. They walked on in silence for maybe half a minute before Matt muttered: 'There.' He was nodding towards a blinking red dot on the corner of Castle Ironworks. The curved gleam of a camera lens was just visible next to it.

'Wait a minute,' said Tima.

They all paused, although Elena hadn't a clue why. 'What is it?' she whispered.

'Shhhh.' Tima held out one hand and then turned it palm up in an elegant, slow movement. She lifted her palm slightly, small fingers outstretched, and then let out a long, slow breath, almost as if she was blowing something away from her.

Elena peered across at the security camera. The gleam of the curved glass lens was now just a tiny chink of light . . . and now . . . nothing. The pinprick of red next to it also flickered and died.

'What are you doing?' Elena breathed.

'They're helping me,' said Tima. She was smiling.

'Who? Who's helping you?' asked Matt, at the other side of Tima.

'The moths,' she said. 'I asked them to cover up the camera for me. And they did.'

Elena felt prickles chasing over her skin as she turned to stare at the girl. 'You're telling me you can talk to *moths*?!'

Tima grinned and shrugged. 'It's no big deal,' she said. 'Matt can talk to birds.'

Matt shook his head. 'Seriously—that was a one-time thing!

I'm not, like, some kind of bird whisperer!'

'Aren't you?' asked Tima. 'How do you know?'

Matt glanced around him. 'There aren't any birds here anyway,' he muttered.

'There are loads of birds here,' said Tima. 'They're just asleep—roosting. On the cliff face, in the bushes and trees. You could probably wake them up if you wanted to.'

Elena had a moment of recall. 'Wait . . . when you said about there being no insects or spiders alive in the warehouse,' she said. 'Is that how you knew? Because you can talk to creepy-crawlies?'

'It's not like we're swapping phone numbers,' said Tima, walking on again now. 'It's only been happening for a week, anyway. It totally freaked me out to start with. Until I met you two I was convinced I was going mad. Literally, going mad. But I'm not the only one, am I? Matt just told us what he did with the starlings.'

'Another camera,' muttered Matt, and Tima paused and went through the whole performance again. This time Elena saw the tiny winged insects pouring along the invisible line she pointed, arriving at the security camera and clustering on it like bees on a honeycomb.

'I've never been so amazed in my life,' Elena said, feeling rather light-headed. If Tima could do this—and maybe Matt could too—*she* might be able to.

'Me neither,' said Tima. 'But I'm getting used to it now. I kind of like it. I probably overdid it with the bee beard, though . . .'

'The bee *what*?' Elena halted and turned to stare at her.

'I was in the garden, and I, kind of, asked the bees to come over. I was thinking about those guys you see on the telly sometimes, you know, who get bees walking all over them.'

'And . . . you got them to land on you?' asked Matt. 'Why would you do *that*?'

'I don't know, but it was fine . . . I mean, I was dripping with bees, and not one of them stung me. It felt quite nice, actually. But then my mum saw it all and totally freaked out. I had to tell her I found the queen and picked her up and the rest of the colony must have followed her. She couldn't believe I was so calm . . . and not stung to death. She nearly phoned pest control, but the bees had all flown off by then.'

'So . . . you're like Doctor Dolittle for insects,' marvelled Elena. She turned to Matt. 'And you've got birds!'

'There's got to be a reason this is happening to us,' said Matt, shaking his head. 'I want to know. This is messing with my mind. Let's get to this warehouse and see if there's anything going on there.'

Tima did her moth dance twice more before they got to the corner of Quarry End where the Sentry SuperSacks warehouse stood tall and silent. Really, really silent.

Elena wondered if she was imagining it because of what Tima had told her, but it did seem like an unearthly quiet surrounded the building. It was brick-built on the ground floor level, and then corrugated steel ran right up to its flat, gently angled roof. It was taller than her house.

'Is this it?' asked Matt.

'Yes,' said Tima. 'Can you hear it?'

'Hear what?'

'Nothing.'

Matt stood listening for several seconds and then nodded. 'It's like digital silence,' he said. 'The kind of silence they put on music recordings in between tracks . . . no atmos. Nothing.'

Elena shivered, not for the first time that night. She thought she saw movement in every shadow—twice she had glanced back over her shoulder, convinced there was a dark shape flitting away behind them—but she didn't hear *a thing*. She gulped and said: 'Are we going in, then? Do you want to get your mothy mates to block up the cameras again?'

'Already done it,' said Tima. 'I don't need to ask any more. They've got the idea now. Anything bright, flickering, or pulsing on that building, they're all over it.'

'OK . . . but can any of them break a padlock?' asked Matt as they approached the trade office entrance of the warehouse. There wasn't a padlock, in fact—just a firmly locked, white PVC door.

'I think breaking and entering is pushing it for a mob of moths,' said Tima. 'But they can probably show us any weak points—where we might get in. I'll ask them to look.'

A flickering cloud above their head began to take form. In seconds it was all around the building. A curtain of shimmering night insects descended on the crack along the top of the huge roll-open doors at the front end. Tima shook her head. 'Too high,' she said. Then a funnel of tiny winged beasts began to loop and swirl away from the front and around the side. It probed, like a ghostly finger, far along the right-hand flank of the building—close to the dark face of the quarry cliff. 'There!' said Tima, triumphantly. 'See!'

They ran down the narrow concrete strip towards it and found a window at head height. It was frosted, and only the top part of it was open. Moths and other flying night insects were swooping in and out of the thin gap. 'Thank you,' said their employer, and they cleared the area at once. Tima got a slim pen torch out of her jeans pocket and switched it on. 'No,' she said, as several winged friends made for the beam of light. 'Not this one.' They departed instantly. 'Boost me up!' she said. 'I can look through.'

'It smells like a toilet,' said Elena, catching the scent of soap and disinfectant through the shallow window. She and Matt boosted up lightweight Tima easily, and the girl pulled the small window wider and then wriggled through it as far as her waist, flashing the torchlight around on the other side. There was a scrape and a clunk, and then the bigger, lower window swung open. Tima slid awkwardly back out of the top window and then swung through the lower one like a gymnast. 'It is a toilet,' she called back. 'Come on in.'

Elena shivered. She wasn't *at all* sure she wanted to go inside that silent warehouse.

'C'mon,' said Matt, getting ready to boost her up. 'It was *your* idea.'

That did it. *Damn right,* it was her idea. And she was going *in*!

CHAPTER 15

Matt clambered through the window last, scraping his shoulder on the thin metal frame and landing on the tiled floor with a thud. It was a toilet, with two cubicles, a store cupboard and a couple of sinks. The girls were looking around by the skinny light of Tima's torch and the thicker beam of a bigger torch Elena had pulled out of her backpack. Several moths were fluttering in the beams. Tima shone her torch back to the open window and said, 'Out there,' and the creatures flew out in single file, like jets departing Heathrow. Matt stared at her in awe. Could *he* do that with starlings? The thought made him shiver.

'Come on,' he said. 'I'm not standing around in the bog all night. If we're going to look for something, let's . . . *look* for something.' He pushed open the door, and they found themselves in a narrow corridor with breeze-block walls and a concrete floor. 'Have you got a plan?' he asked Elena. 'Any particular place to go?'

Elena frowned in the torchlight. 'The man who was carrying the box of dead birds . . . I think he said they'd flown right through to the back of the warehouse. So . . . let's go there.'

They found doors off to a couple of rooms—an office and a small kitchen—to their left and then a large double door on their right. Matt half expected it to be locked, but as he pushed the handle down the first of the double doors swung open. 'Wait—you might want this,' said Elena, at his side. She handed him a spare torch from her sensible little backpack. He bet she had a first aid kit in there too. He nodded and grunted his thanks, not wanting to voice what he was thinking: that he was a lamebrain for not bringing a torch of his own. Truth was, he'd imagined using the light from his mobile phone . . . forgetting that he no longer possessed one.

He pushed through the doors and into the darkness of the warehouse.

Immediately the air changed. It wasn't just the slightly buttery smell of paper and bubble wrap and cardboard. There was something else he couldn't put his finger on. Something very faint . . . like spoiled meat in an old fridge.

And then there was that heavy stillness. It was partly the natural acoustics, of course. Shelf after shelf of padded envelopes and cardboard was bound to dampen the sound. And yet, like Tima said, it seemed so, *so* dead.

'Do you think we could put a light on?' whispered Tima. She was standing a little closer to him, and Matt realized he wasn't alone in feeling scared.

'Too risky,' he said, putting a hand on her shoulder in a manner that surprised him. Being a comforting presence to anyone was entirely new. *Menacing* presence had always been more his thing. 'Might get seen from outside. The tops of the big doors at the front weren't sealed properly, were they? Your moth army showed us.'

'True,' said Tima. 'Although they're more moth RAF, I think,' she added.

Elena took a breath, stepped out, and then turned right, following the straight beam of her torch along the first alleyway, towards the back of the warehouse. On either side of her, shelves of stationery towered to the height of a house. Matt hastened after her. He didn't want to be the 'bringing up the rear' guy. Tima stayed hot on his heels, clearly feeling the same way.

It took perhaps 20 seconds to reach the far end of the warehouse to find . . . nothing. Just a warehouse wall and yet more shelving. At the midpoint, though, was a stretch of naked grey breeze blocks. A single black fire escape door was set into it.

Matt felt a slight crunch beneath his trainers and angled the borrowed torch downward. He flinched when he saw he was standing on a pile of insects and spiders. They were mostly dead; one or two of them were still feebly moving a wing or a feeler. 'Look at this,' he hissed.

There was silence, and then he looked up to see Tima and Elena shining the torch closer to the wall. 'Look at *this*,' said Elena. At her feet were several birds. Three of them were clearly dead, and two were still moving.

Matt ran across the crunching insect carpet and knelt down beside the birds. Two rooks, a starling, and a couple of pigeons. The starling and one pigeon were still alive, but too feeble to do more than shiver and slightly work their beaks as he crouched over them. Matt, his heart thudding almost painfully, shoved his torch into the waistband of his jeans and picked up the starling. It slumped between his hands, raising its head once as if to look at him, and then letting it flop back again. 'I need to get it out of here,' he said. 'Bring the other one!'

A sudden urgency shoved him to his feet, and he found himself running back down the alleyway and round to the door, the torchlight dancing randomly out of his waistband and flashing in all directions. When he reached the window they'd climbed in through he scrambled up and through it with only one hand, keeping the other cupped against his chest, cradling the dying bird.

He knelt on the narrow concrete path and gently laid the starling down, dimly aware of Tima and Elena climbing out behind him. He rested the torch next to the bird, and it sent its beam in a narrow shaft along the pavement. Tima knelt next to him and placed the pigeon beside the starling. 'Will they make it?' she asked.

Matt shook his head. He could feel the life force draining out of both the starling and the pigeon. *What happened to you?* he asked them, in his head. *Why did you go in there? And why couldn't you get out?*

The starling lifted its head to look at him, and goosebumps rose all over his skin. Was this the bird he'd made eye contact with at the car wash? *Could* it be? It seemed to *know* him. *I'm sorry,* he sent. *I don't know how to save you. What happened to you? Why did you all fly in there?*

The starling rested its head back on to the concrete and then, with what must have been its last tiny flame of energy, it moved one wing. The iridescent feathers swam under Matt's eyes, and he realized he was crying. The wing spread like a fan, opening up and sending its tip into the path of the torchlight. The starling rolled its head once more, its bead-like eyes connecting with Matt's, and then it sank to the ground for the last time. The light left the eyes. The wing stayed put. Matt felt a sob shake his chest, and he bunched his fist and put it against his mouth. No crying. No crying in front of girls.

'They were trying to tell you,' said Tima, her voice soft nearby.

Only then did Matt look at the pigeon. Only then did he realize the other bird had made the exact same movement with its wing. Both of them lay dead now. And both of them were pointing a wing tip into the beam of light.

Matt sniffed, coughed, and got to his feet. 'It doesn't make any sense!'

Tima touched his arm. 'It does. You just need to work it out.'

'They were both pointing at the torchlight,' said Elena. 'So . . . it's something to do with light . . . ? Maybe . . . ? Maybe there's a big light in there that was switched on earlier— attracting them in.'

Tima shook her head. 'No. It's not the light. Birds don't do that flying at the light thing, do they? And these birds don't fly at night. They roost at sunset. So, why . . . ?'

91

'We're here too late,' said Matt. 'It all happened before we got here.'

'So . . . when *should* we have been here?' asked Elena.

'Isn't it obvious?' he said. 'One thirty-four! If this is connected to us, then we know what time it all kicks off, don't we? One thirty-four in the morning.'

They were silent for a moment, and Elena nodded her head. 'So tomorrow, we need to set an alarm for half past midnight. We need to be *here* at one thirty-four. Watching what happens.'

'OK,' said Tima. 'Let's do that. We can't do any more here now, can we?' She sounded tired and a little shaky, and Matt remembered that she was still a little kid—only ten.

'You're right,' he said. 'Time to go.'

They closed the lower toilet window from the outside, and then Matt boosted Tima back up so she could reach down through the narrow top window again, this time fastening the handle on the other side. 'We might as well not give away that we've been inside,' said Matt. They pushed the upper window mostly closed as it had been before.

Matt bent down to pick up the dead birds before they left, then gave a small cry of surprise. 'Look at this . . .' he said, turning to them. 'Their eyes.' In his hands, their fine, light skulls cradled in his fingers, both birds were staring blankly into the night; their eyes were flatly gleaming . . . and *red*.

'What *is* that?' murmured Elena, peering more closely.

'Animal eyes sometimes look red in the dark,' said Tima. 'They reflect.'

'This doesn't look like that,' said Elena, peering closer still.

'They're not reflecting. They're just . . . red. Maybe it's blood or something.' She shivered visibly.

Matt shook his head. 'Whatever . . . I can't just leave them here to be dumped in the bin. I'll put them somewhere better.' On the outer corner of the warehouse, just where the side alley began, was a clump of bushes with thick waxy leaves. Matt carried the birds here and deposited them with care, deep into the undergrowth. Their delicate feathered frames, already cooling, slid silently into the shadow of the leaves. It was better than concrete. Or a bin.

Matt gave his eyes a fierce wipe before he rejoined Elena and Tima, and then they quietly made their way back across the estate. Tima's moth RAF did duty again, once more blocking the security cameras. 'I think that's officially a superpower,' Elena murmured, patting the younger girl's shoulder. 'Incredible.'

The digits on Matt's watch showed 4.13. Dawn was close. Would he get an hour or two of sleep when he got back? He wouldn't have to do car wash duty until eleven on Sunday—so he might sleep. He *might*.

Getting back over the fence wasn't easy. They hadn't thought it through. There were no bins on this side to give them a step up to the roof of the booth. Scouting around, they found an old trailer, unattached, resting near the ironworks. One of its two tyres was flat, but it rolled along OK when they each took a bit and shoved. Matt pinned the tow bar down, standing on it to keep it steady, while Elena climbed up from the top end of it and then hauled Tima up. It see-sawed up again when he let go of the tow bar and climbed along it himself. It wasn't going to be easy. But Elena and Tima lay flat on their bellies on the roof of the booth and grabbed him as he launched himself up. He came close to dragging the pair of them back down but just managed to get a proper anchor on the flat fibreglass roof, scrabbling his trainers against the side.

Getting down on to the skip was no problem, and jumping to the ground from that was easier still. 'We need to put this back where it was,' said Matt, giving the skip a shove. 'If they work out there've been people over the fence they might get some security guys over.'

'What about *that*?' Tima pointed to the trailer on the far side of the booth.

Matt shrugged. 'Can't do anything about that,' he said. 'But maybe they'll think someone just left it there. Maybe.' He knew he should have come better prepared. Tomorrow night he would.

They walked Tima home first, making plans to meet again at the bandstand the next night, only this time at a quarter to one. A short walk from her house Tima suddenly hugged them both in turn. 'I don't know what's happening,' she whispered. 'And it's scary and, I think, maybe dangerous . . . but I'm so glad we're all in this. I'm so glad I met you!' Then she fled around the corner and into her house.

Matt and Elena stood in silence for a while. At length Matt said: 'She's a bit . . .'

'Yeah,' said Elena. 'But that's OK. One of us has to be.' She gave him a slightly wonky grin.

He walked her home, watching as she let herself into the small terraced house. She didn't creep in, he noticed. She used her key confidently, gave him a little wave, and went straight inside. He wondered if her parents were even there.

Then he went back to his place: the neat, tidy, stress-filled little flat above the car wash. He slowed his walk as he approached and stared up at the dark windows.

It's OK, he told himself. *He'll be asleep.*

CHAPTER 16

Elena searched through the bureau in the sitting room until she found the maps. If she'd lived in a normal house she would have been on the family laptop doing all this with just the rattle of a few keys, but Mum had let the broadband package lapse months ago. They got a few Freeview channels on the TV, and they had a landline phone and a mobile each, but she had no wi-fi here and no printer. And Mum's old laptop lay under a thin blanket of dust beneath her bed. She had tried to get Mum to get the broadband service back online again, but Mum said enough bad news came through the few channels they *did* have. She didn't want to let any more in.

Still, the map would do the job. As the dawn light filtered through the curtains, she sat at the dining table, switched the lamp on, and spread out the map of Thornleigh. Google would have pinpointed the exact dwellings she was looking for. The paper version was not so helpful, but she could still work out fairly accurately where Tima's house was, midway along Cheriton Place, and she knew that Kowski Kar Klean was right on the bend of Mulberry Road. Her own road, Jenkin Way, was a long line of small terraced houses. She and Mum lived three houses in from the end of the road.

She ran her flattened palms across the map, seeing again the birds, each spreading out one wing with their last breath of life, pointing to the straight pathway of light from the torch.

She returned to the bureau for a pencil and a ruler. Back at the table she carefully placed the right-angled tip of one end of the ruler on Kowski Kar Klean and, pinning it down with her finger, moved the other end in an arc until it fell across Tima's house. The direct line ran roughly north-west to south-east as far as she could tell. She marked it lightly in pencil and then stared for a few moments, before blinking away her disbelief. About equidistant between her new friends' homes lay Jenkin Way. If she was not mistaken, her house lay right on that pencil line. The room around her seemed to hum with significance.

Taking a deep breath, she slid the ruler along, true to her pencil line, like a flat plastic train. Beyond Tima's house and further south-east, travelling on at precisely the same angle—she knew it even before the train arrived. The next stop was Quarry End.

CHAPTER 17

He stood in the safe shelter of a clump of holly bushes and watched the lamplight filtering through the downstairs curtains. She was still up. She hadn't gone to bed. Even though it was almost dawn.

Time was running out. He'd never stayed out this late before, but, hey, he'd never had this much entertainment before. What were they *doing*? Why had they broken into a warehouse in the middle of the night and then come out with nothing but two dying birds?

He'd been intending to mess with them. He nearly had, a couple of times, but then something stopped him—fascination. They were just so unlikely a trio—Car-wash Boy, Tiny Dancer, and Good Girl. How on earth had they ever hooked up together? They were from different parts of town and even though the older two went to the same school you had only to look at them to realize they would NEVER be friends. Not in ordinary circumstances. She, so neat and well-behaved—he, so rough and resentful. And Tiny Dancer was from RichToffsVille and went to the prep school. Her parents would throw a *fit* if they knew she'd been hanging out with the riff-raff from the local state school.

But these were clearly not ordinary circumstances. He'd thought the night walks would fizzle out, but they seemed to be going strong. Why? Some kind of insomniac support group? Except there was something else going on with them. That *thing* with the moths . . . He shivered again; an uncommon sensation. It was rare that *anything* spooked him. '*I* am the one who spooks,' he muttered.

The light began to tickle at him. He cursed. He was not done watching and thinking. Ever since he'd spotted Good Girl, gazing calmly out into the night, framed in her window like the Mona Lisa, things had changed. He had messed with her mind, but then found the only messed-up mind was *his*. This wasn't how it was meant to go.

OK. Enough. The tickle was turning to a burn. No time left to stand and stare. Tonight he would get on to the roof of the bandstand, lie back, and wait for their next meeting—listen in properly.

Dawn light suddenly washed the street. It was like a punch in the face. He wrapped his black cotton cowl around his head and ran.

CHAPTER 18

'Tima—you have a visitor,' said Mum, smiling and raising her eyebrows. Clearly it was not a visitor she had been expecting. 'Come on through,' she said, to the visitor.

Tima looked up from her book and blinked in surprise. It was her music teacher. Mr James waved, looking oddly out of place in their house instead of next to a piano in the music studio at school. She put her book aside and smiled.

'Tima!' he called. 'You're looking a lot better! How are you?'

'I'll get tea,' said Mum, and went into the kitchen.

'I *am* better,' said Tima and was surprised to realize it was true. After last night's excursion to Quarry End and all the drama with the dead birds, she should be exhausted. As it turned out she'd come home, got into bed, and fallen asleep almost immediately. She reckoned she might have got as much as six hours altogether.

She no longer felt like she might tip over at any moment.

'Good,' said Mr James, with a wide smile. He sat down on the sofa opposite. 'We really missed you in the show, you know.'

Tima felt a twist inside. It still hurt—badly—to think of how she'd screwed everything up. Tomorrow she would have to go back to school and face Lily and her mates and all their fake sympathy. She was not looking forward to it, and the plan to meet Elena and Matt again tonight was the only thing that was really keeping her mind off it.

'Thing is,' Mr James went on, 'you had a tough time of it. You crashed out of the show because you weren't well—and you might be thinking that's the last time you put yourself up on stage.'

Tima nodded. *Spot on, Mr James. Never again.*

'Thing is, Tima—you *have* to.'

'I *do*?'

'Yes,' he replied, smiling still, but with an underlying expression of stony determination. 'When you fall off a bike, you have to get straight back on—or you'll spend all your life being frightened of cycling, when you could be out there having a whale of a time on two wheels. It's the same with performance. You had a bad experience ... but try to remember all the *good* experiences. Remember the church service at Christmas, when you sang the solo. How did that go?'

She found herself grinning as she remembered. It had been wonderful. Her year group and their families had all crowded into St Thomas's Church, round the corner from the school. It was a pretty church with high vaulted ceilings and amazing acoustics. As a girl with Arab parents, it was perhaps odd that she should be there, but Mum and Dad weren't very religious, and they loved to hear her sing anything. In the church there was no need for a microphone. When she sang her solo she had felt as if her voice was carrying up to the stars. It had been 'When a Child is Born'; a Christmas song with a melody that rose and fell like a lark on the wing. The song had poured out of her throat and flown up and up as the audience listened in rapt attention. The hairs on her arms and shoulders had prickled at the delight of hitting every note perfectly. She had still been so new at school and so nervous at the start, but the adrenaline had only powered up her performance to a new level. It had been joyous.

When she finished, there was a moment of silence and then the whole church had erupted with applause and even some whooping. It was a bit improper for a school church service. Mr James had stood up at the piano and joined in with the applause, looking immensely proud of her.

'Yes—I remember,' she said.

'Good,' said her teacher. '*That's* what you need to do. Remember the good stuff. And think of all the rehearsals for *Oliver!* we had when you were having such a ball. I *know* . . .' he paused and looked at her meaningfully, ' . . . Lily and her friends were giving you a hard time.'

Tima's eyebrows shot up. He'd *noticed*?

'And I know what Lily can be like,' he went on. 'But even with all of that to deal with, you were loving it, weren't you?'

She nodded. The rehearsals had been the highlight of every week. She'd got a great buzz out of watching the others too. One or two of her fellow performers were really good—funny and clever. It was fascinating to see how their confidence grew under the direction of Mrs Theroux; how they all improved; blocking out their moves on the stage, brushing up their dialogue, working on their dance routines and their harmonies. Pulling together to make something fantastic happen on stage was wonderful. She *had* loved being part of it.

'So—I have a proposal for you,' said Mr James. 'I thought it might help to talk to you before you come back to school tomorrow.'

'OK . . .' said Tima, feeling nervous and intrigued. Mum arrived at that point, carrying a tray of tea and biscuits. She sat down next to Mr James and put the tray on the coffee table.

'Go on,' she said. 'We're all ears!'

'We've been asked to do a short performance for a charity event,' said Mr James. 'It's on Wednesday night at Thornleigh Town Hall—they had something else planned, but the entertainment they'd booked pulled out. So they'd like us to stage two or three scenes from *Oliver!*, including song and dance routines.'

'Oh,' said Tima, feeling suddenly breathless.

'I'd like to do the big crowd-pleaser—"Consider Yourself" went on Mr James. 'And then "Pick a Pocket" . . . and finish up with "As Long as He Needs Me".'

Tima gulped. That was her big song. Well . . . *Lily's* big song, as it had turned out.

'So . . . are you up for it?'

Tima stared at him, feeling her face flush with excitement. Or was it fear? She couldn't be sure. 'What . . . what about Lily?

Shouldn't you be asking her? I mean, she took over, didn't she? And I heard she did really well and there's an agent interested in her and everything.'

'Who told you that?' he asked, raising one sceptical eyebrow. Then he laughed and added: 'Let me guess . . . Lily?'

Tima shrugged and giggled. 'Um . . . yeah.'

'Lily will be in it too,' he said. 'As Bet—not Nancy. She won't like it, but I'm sure she'll understand why it's a great idea to let you get back up and try again.'

'That sounds fantastic,' said Mum. 'I'm sure Tima wants to do it . . . don't you, sweetheart?'

Tima thought about it. What if she froze again? What if everything went wrong? This time in front of not just the school hall—the whole *town hall*? It was a huge risk—but part of her was fizzing with delight. She *could* do it this time. She was stronger now—much more in control, since she'd met Elena and Matt. And it would be so lovely to finally sing out her role and get it right.

'OK,' she said. 'I'll do it.'

Mr James beamed. Then gave a huge sigh. 'Thank goodness for that!' he said and glanced across at Mum. 'Strictly between ourselves, I wasn't going to say yes to the town hall event if Tima said no. The person who asked us to get involved heard her sing at Christmas . . . It was only a done deal with Tima as Nancy.'

'Wow,' said Tima. She couldn't think of anything to add.

'Needless to say,' said Mr James after a gulp of tea. '*That* stays between us!'

Mum showed him out a short while later, chatting happily

to him about the upcoming show and how Tima would be more than ready for it. As she closed the door behind him she turned and beamed at her daughter.

'Tima—that is *such* good news. It's exactly what you need. This time you'll absolutely smash it. I know you will.'

Tima said, 'Thanks . . . I'm going to give it my best shot. I think I'll be OK.'

Mum nodded slowly and let out a long breath. 'And maybe . . . no more talking to bees?'

'Mum—I told you, I picked up the queen and . . .'

'I know,' said Mum. 'I understand how it happened; I've looked it up online. What I don't understand is *why*. You've always been so nervous around insects, and all of a sudden, there you are sitting there, cool as a cucumber, as thousands of bees crawl all over you.' She shuddered.

'I've just chilled out a bit,' said Tima. 'After what happened on stage last week, things like *insects* just don't matter.' She knew it was a lame explanation. She couldn't think of anything else to say.

'Something's going on with you,' said Mum, running her thumb down her daughter's cheek. 'There are shadows under your eyes. You're still not sleeping properly, are you?'

'It's all much better than it was,' Tima said, at least half truthfully. 'Honestly—I'm fine. I'm *weird*, true, but you knew that already.'

Mum ruffled her hair. 'You're amazing,' she said. 'I'm booking you a brain scan.'

CHAPTER 19

When his alarm went off at midnight, Matt jolted out of sleep, confused. He'd been in the middle of a dream where a starling was chalking a message for him on the damp concrete floor of the car wash, holding the stubby white stick in its beak.

Matt sat up, silenced the alarm clock, and rubbed his face, trying to remember what the message was. It was slipping away from his memory like water through his fingers. Something to do with light and dark . . .

He got up, shaking sleep out of his head, and the dream with it. He quickly dressed, his heart speeding up with excitement. Maybe tonight they were going to find out the cause of their sleeplessness. They'd be a lot slicker getting in and out of there too, now. He had worked out a system, and everything he needed was stowed behind the car wash supplies shed. All afternoon yesterday, he'd washed cars on autopilot, exchanging not a word with his father except the odd grunt and nod. As he automatically doused, soaped, washed, dried, and waxed, he had been totally focused on the problem of a much easier break-in.

For a start, they needed to get Tima's moths to cluster around those tall orange street lights and dim everything down a bit. Three kids were just too easy to see in that glare. Quarry End was in a cul-de-sac, so there weren't any cars passing by, but that didn't mean people weren't about. Someone *might* be pulling an all-nighter in one of the units—or down the road at the power plant; you never knew. More than once last night he had thought someone was following them. It was just his nerves, of course, but that didn't mean it was impossible. In lower light he'd feel a lot safer.

Next they needed to scale the fence and get in over the security booth like before—and then out again. If the trailer they'd used to get out before had been moved back to its original parking space, it would *definitely* raise suspicion if they rolled it back to the booth and left it behind in the same position for a second night running. They needed a better plan.

He had it all worked out by the time he and Dad had finished at teatime. He ate with his parents and then excused himself and slipped out into the car wash to find what he needed. Dad had settled down to watch football and drink lager, and, once that started, nothing would distract him. In better times, Matt would sometimes join him. Mum too, on occasion. Lager didn't seem to make his father as angry as spirits, and he was sometimes even quite nice—especially if his team was winning. After the Xbox incident, though, Matt thought it would be a very long time before he joined Dad on the sofa to watch footie. It occurred to him there were little invisible strings that bound people to their family. Some of them would stay intact, come what may. But not all of them. One of the invisible strings between himself and his father had snapped yesterday. Permanently.

Maybe it was for the best. He'd decided some time ago to leave home the minute he turned 16, if he possibly could. Maybe sign up for the Navy, like Ben. It would be easier with fewer of those invisible strings.

All was dark and quiet in the flat as he opened his bedroom door. He stood for a few moments, listening. Then he stepped out, and a second later there was a crash and he was shoved sideways.

'Whoa!' he yelled, unable to stop. His father loomed over him.

'Whoa—mind yourself,' exclaimed the lumbering figure. The door to the bathroom was rebounding. 'Whachudoinup?' enquired his father as he reached his and Mum's bedroom. He was wearing only boxers as far as Matt could see. The belly he'd grown, with the help of a thousand beers, shook like jelly.

'Just going myself,' Matt muttered, nodding towards the bathroom and hoping Dad was too far gone to notice his son was fully dressed.

'Aright. Night then,' burbled his old man. 'Nice car work today, nipper. More sleep, see? Betterforyou . . .'

'Yeah,' breathed Matt.

Dad shut the bedroom door and once again, silence reigned.

Matt visited the toilet—partly to be convincing, but also partly because after that fright, he needed to. When he came back out again Dad's muffled snores reassured him. He quietly let himself out of the flat and went down to the car wash. Behind the store he picked up a large backpack. Its contents were more bulky than heavy, but he was pleased to have them with him. The system was good. It would work. It would be satisfying to show Elena and Tima that he could do more than sniffle over dead birds.

He shouldered the backpack, pulled up the hood of his top, and set out for Tima's bandstand. He was still jangling and nervy after the encounter with his dad. He expected at any moment to feel a hand grab his shoulder with a demand to know where the hell he was going. But Dad didn't follow him—and there seemed to be nobody else about. A car passed once, headlights giving ample warning of its approach, and he stepped into the shadow of a bus shelter until it had gone.

Halfway to the bandstand something pale glided down from an overhang of oak trees. Matt held his breath. What was it? It circled some houses and then swooped back, lower this time. It was a barn owl ... luminous and ghostly. Matt felt a tingling in his spine. Could he ... could he communicate with it?

The owl flew towards him and silently passed so low that he felt the downdraught of its wings on his face. Then it was gone, lost in the dark oaks. Could he call it back?

Don't be so daft, said a cynical voice inside him. *You're not some kind of bird whisperer. Try it and you'll fail and be angry when you meet Elena and Tima. Leave it.*

Matt left it.

CHAPTER 20

They arrived at Quarry End in silence. Pausing beneath a clump of holly trees across the road from the main entrance, they stared across at the familiar empty security booth, beside the metal gates.

Elena turned and pointed back the way they'd come. She held her arm straight and still. 'Along this line,' she said, 'you will find Tima's house. Keep going and it hits *my* house. Go on a bit further and guess what?'

'*My* place,' said Matt.

He didn't look convinced, so she showed them both the map again, with its straight pencil mark. 'Look—it runs north-west to south-east. Straight as my ruler. Don't you think that's weird?' They nodded, and she shivered. It wasn't altogether an unpleasant sensation. She was excited. It was hard to imagine that just a few days ago she'd never even spoken to Matt or

Tima. Why they were connected like this, she had no clue, but if this all ended tonight . . . she'd miss them. Somehow, though, she didn't think it was going to end tonight.

'So, you reckon it goes straight through there,' Matt waved towards the gates, 'and right into that packaging warehouse?'

'Yes,' said Elena. 'I do. I just wish I had a compass I could use to be sure.'

'Your phone,' said Matt. 'There'll be a compass app on it.' He tried, and failed, to not look bitter. His own phone was still confiscated.

'Oh! I didn't think of that! Where's the compass?' said Elena, pulling out her mobile. She accessed the main screen and peered at the apps on it. 'Where is it?' Matt sighed heavily and plonked a finger down on the little compass icon. 'Oh! Has it always been there? You know, I never even noticed.'

'Girls!' groaned Matt. 'Seriously!'

'Don't you gender stereotype *me*!' snapped Tima.

Elena laughed aloud. 'You tell him, titch!' she grinned. 'Now, shut up, both of you. Let's get over the fence and track the beam with my compass.'

'First, get your moths to work,' Matt said to Tima. 'It's way too bright over there. Get them to cover up the street lights. And all the security cameras, like before. Are there enough of them?'

'There are thousands of them,' said Tima. 'Millions.'

'Tell them,' said Matt.

'I don't tell them,' said Tima. 'I ask. You can't tell them, Matt. It's a request, not an order.'

111

'Whatever,' he grunted. 'Just make it happen.'

Tima looked around her. So far tonight, Elena had not noticed any moths following the girl. She had even wondered whether they'd given up trailing her—but apparently not. Tima stepped out of the shadow of the holly trees and lifted her arms like a ballet dancer. She closed her eyes and smiled and then let out one of those long breaths, gently pursing her lips and almost blowing. Within seconds, a mist of tiny winged creatures began to drift out from the greenery behind them, taking flight from trees and bushes and the craggy overhangs of the quarry cliff face. The mists became swirls, and the swirls travelled up and out and funnelled towards the tall lights.

Elena stared, open-mouthed, at the nearest street light. For a moment the swirl corkscrewed beneath it as if dangling from the lamp, and then it condensed into a darkening orb as their winged helpers amassed on the glass. Across the industrial park the other lights darkened. Soon there was hardly a glimmer of light left. The whole estate became dim. Matt hoisted the large backpack on to his shoulder and set out for the gate.

Elena ran towards the skip, ready to roll it across once more.

'Leave it,' Matt called after her. 'Don't need it.' He stopped beside the gates and dropped the bag at his feet. It was large and khaki green—like an army rucksack—and from it he tipped something rectangular and pale. Elena got out her torch and played the light on to him as he lifted it up. He stood and gave it a shake, and with a sharp whispering rattle it transformed into a skinny ladder. 'Portable—telescopic,' he said. 'Aluminium—so it's light. Stacks away inside itself. We use them at the car wash.

You have to get up high for some of the vans.'

'That's brilliant,' said Elena. 'But . . . how will we get across *that* without a punctured kidney?' She pointed at the vicious spikes along the top of the gate and the fence on either side.

Matt pulled something else out of the bag—a rainbow-shaped arc of thick black rubber. 'I sliced up an old tyre,' he explained. 'This should be tough enough to cover up the spikes as we climb over.'

He set up the ladder. It had soft foam pads at the top, obviously designed for resting against a van's bodywork without scratching. He leaned it against the gate, which was more stable than the metal mesh fence. The ladder reached two-thirds of the way up. Matt climbed it and placed the slice of tyre across the spikes, its curved rubber walls hanging down on either side. He thumped it once or twice, but it seemed securely in place, offering plenty of safe climb-over surface.

'Shall I go first?' asked Tima, making for the ladder.

'Whoa—not yet!' said Matt. He reached into the bag a third time and pulled out some thin, strong rope. He tied one end to the top rung on one side, knotting it tightly, and then tied the other end to the top rung's other corner, making a long loop. It looked like a stepladder shoulder bag, thought Elena, as Matt flung the top of the loop over the gate. She should send the design to Fendi or Chanel.

But this was far more useful. Matt went over first, the rucksack on his back, and then dropped to the concrete on the other side of the gate where he waited to help Tima and Elena down. Once all three were inside he reached up and pulled gently on the loop of rope. With a few coughs and creaks, the aluminium ladder rose up, shuffled on to the tyre, slid across it—pivoted for a moment—and then rapidly slid down towards them. They were all ready to catch it. Nothing hit the floor. No big crash gave them away. Then Matt leaned it back up against the gate and nipped up to collect the tyre off the top.

'That *is* neat,' said Elena, as he collapsed the ladder and stowed it back in the rucksack with the rope and the tyre. 'I'm impressed.'

'Me too,' said Tima. 'Clever stuff.'

Matt scowled up at them both as if they were making fun of him. When he realized they weren't, he shrugged, and let the scowl melt as he hid the rucksack behind a nearby pile of wooden pallets. Elena wondered how often someone told him he was clever. Rarely, was her guess. 'Good call,' she added. 'See—someone rolled the trailer back yesterday.' The trailer had been returned to its spot outside the nearby warehouse. 'They'd definitely be suspicious if it ended up back here again. But we can use your ladder and leave no clue behind. Excellent!'

This time he did smile. It suited him, thought Elena. Shame he didn't do it more often.

'OK,' she said, getting the phone compass working again. 'Look—here's the line.' She pointed back through the gate, the way they'd come. 'And it goes . . .' she angled her body and held her left arm out straight, in line with due south-east, ' . . . right through there.'

She lifted her face to peer through the moth-induced gloom and at once felt a tingle across her shoulders. Yes. Directly in

the path she was pointing out—way down at the far end—was
Sentry SuperSacks.

They walked along behind her, in a line. Nobody said a word
as they approached the warehouse. The invisible beam projecting
from Elena's compass app ran right through the warehouse's
huge double-door entrance at a slight angle. They came to a
halt just in front of it. Matt thudded his open palm against the
tall wooden door. 'So now what? Do we go back in again ... or
do we wait here?' He looked at his watch. 'We've got fourteen
minutes.'

Elena and Tima glanced at each other.

'I don't want to go back in that dead place,' said Tima,
wrapping her arms around herself.

'Nor do I,' said Elena. 'But ... we need to see what's
happening *inside*. Whatever happens, it's in there, where we
found the birds yesterday.'

'C'mon then,' said Matt. 'We haven't got time to wait
around. Are your moth mates still on the security cameras,
Tima?'

Tima smiled and nodded. 'They won't let us down.'

Elena was worried that the toilet window might be properly
shut this time, but it wasn't. It was pushed shut, as they'd left
it the night before, but nobody had thought to latch it on the
inside. Once again, Tima wriggled through and let them in, and
minutes later they were back in the main warehouse, standing by
the fire door at the back, staring at ... nothing.

The carpet of insects and spiders that Matt had discovered
last night had been swept away. There were no birds here, dead

115

or alive. It was just the three of them. They set their torches down on the floor and waited.

'How long now?' whispered Tima, rubbing her arms, although it wasn't cold.

'One minute forty seconds,' said Elena, in the dim glow of her mobile. She tucked it away in her pocket and stood still.

They waited in silence as the seconds ticked by.

'We might not see anything at all,' whispered Tima, as the last minute counted down. 'It might be invisible. We might not . . .'

There was a sound—a whirring—a buzzing. They all spun around and Matt grabbed his torch and shone it in the direction of the noise: the front of the warehouse, above the double doors. The gap the moths had shown them last night was dimly marked out by a long line of pale starlight and, increasingly, the orange glow of the street lights. Tima's moths had probably eased up on their duty now that their mistress and her friends were safely indoors, thought Elena, grabbing her own torch now.

Or maybe they'd just come to join in—because there were definitely flying insects in here now. Flies and beetles and moths were tipping through the gap and dropping into a cloud. It was like a bizarre insect waterfall, twinkling in the light of their torches.

Now the thrumming, flapping sound began to make sense—birds were coming too. Not many—perhaps a dozen—had also flown through the gap above the doors and were swooping and fluttering around the light fittings, high up in the ceiling space among the ducting and metal strut rafters.

None of these flying creatures seemed to have a plan. They all seemed to be waiting for—

Elena felt every hair on her skin suddenly rise up as a massive shiver shook her from head to toe. Across from her Tima gave a small cry and Matt sucked in a sharp breath. Elena felt gripped by some unseen electrical force. The charge was incredibly powerful and yet not painful . . . She found she was unable to move as she heard the song. It arrived like an echo from a far mountain, so sweet and true and golden that her eyes instantly filled with tears.

But not so much that she did not see it.

The beam of light was the colour of amber, pulsing with bubbles, twists, and curls of blue, green, and gold. It shot across the warehouse on a gentle slope, flowing straight through the front doors and across to the wall above the fire escape at the back. Later, Elena would realize that her brain must have slipped into slow motion, because she had time to notice the insects and birds, whirling in after the beam, diving and corkscrewing in its wake, moving towards it as if in ecstasy.

The music was engulfing her completely; if she ever got to Grade 8 in cornet and joined a world-class orchestra and played for monarchs and presidents in the best concert halls around the planet, she could still never be part of such an exquisite sound. If she *touched* that channel of light and musical beauty she might be transported to heaven and never return.

When at last it rang out its final angelic note and the light chased through the breeze-block wall, vanishing like a train into a tunnel, she found she was carolling incoherently after it, not even forming words. Everything inside her simply cried out, '*TAKE ME! TAKE ME WITH YOU!*'

And she wasn't the only one. She could hear the others too ... *all* of them, human and animal. Her eyes closed. When they opened she found herself on the floor, tangled up with Matt and Tima, a heap of insects, and several birds.

She disentangled herself and got to her feet, dazed. The birds were dazed too, but they didn't seem, as she grabbed her torch and cast a trembling light across them, to be hurt. They were getting to their feet, just as Matt and Tima were, looking bewildered. Even the insects were beginning to rally, rising up in clouds.

So ... what had killed the other ones?

Abruptly, the ecstasy left her. A coldness clawed in the pit of her belly. Suddenly she grabbed Tima and Matt by their arms and dragged them away from the fire escape door.

'It's not the beam!' she said. 'It's not the beam. The beam pulls them in ... but it doesn't kill them—it's something ...'

'... else,' said Matt, as the fire escape began to shudder. He shoved Elena and Tima behind him and kept them back with an arm on either side. They didn't fight him, but held on to him, staring across his shoulders, rapt and fearful. Whatever 'else' was, it was coming. Now.

CHAPTER 21

Deadness.

Tima felt it drop through her, a cascade of dread. It felt as if her belly was suddenly full of cold stones. The beautiful, singing golden beam had vanished, and now something else was coming in. Rebounding, maybe, from the loveliness. Something negative to rebalance the world.

A light began to filter around the edges of the fire escape door. Later she would try to describe what colour it was but fail. The best she could do was say ... dark red or blue or purple, but it was none of these ... it was almost an *anti*-light. A light that was somehow *dark*.

Tima felt the fear in Elena and Matt too, and that made her own fear intensify. The birds ... even the insects ... all seemed to be on pause, just like them. Gripped by the dark light. The straight shafts of it began to change as they all stared, frozen to the spot. First they bent, in a way that any normal light, shone through from the other side, simply could not. It snapped the laws of physics in half. The lines of dark light bent and then *writhed* and became something living . . . tentacles reaching out from some unimaginable creature. Something from the deep earth.

There was a sound too. No—more like an *anti*-sound. It was the shock of silence as all sound is abruptly sucked from your ears, leaving only the panicky reverb of your own brain, trying to make sense of it. This would be how it felt to be struck deaf. Tima's logic filter suddenly clogged with the realization that she HAD gone deaf. She flung her hands up to her ears, pummelling at them—and screamed.

No sound. NO SOUND. NO SOUND AT ALL! And still she screamed—only knowing that it WAS a scream because of the vibration across her tongue and throat, the soreness already scraping her voice box.

And still the dark-light tentacles moved, snatching the birds first, pulling them towards the door, where they flapped and silently screamed too, their beaks flung wide and their eyes popping, brilliant with fear in one second, dull, flat red the next.

The insects were dropping lifeless to the floor, but some were escaping. One bird, too, turned and spun away from the tentacles. It flew just above their heads, the downdraught of its wings stirring the air, one wing striking Matt's head.

And this was the moment when Matt moved. He turned and grabbed Tima and Elena and shoved them back along the warehouse corridor.

'—OOVE! MOVE! MOVE!!!'

His words shot through Tima's ears like cannon fire as her hearing abruptly returned. Her own scream tailed off to be replaced by jagged, hitching breaths and gulps as she tore along the narrow corridor of packets and bubble wrap. At the end, Matt dragged her left and along to the side doors they'd entered by. Elena was running ahead. She flung the doors open in time for her friends to pelt through.

As the doors swung shut behind them they did not stop. They were back in the toilet, up on the sill, and through the window in seconds. They each landed on the narrow paved walkway and sprinted back to the front of the building. Tima would have kept on sprinting too—right to the fence and the ladder and the safety beyond, but Matt caught hold of her again and pulled her to a halt. Elena stopped too. For a while they could not speak; only drag in tearing breaths, bent over double, hands on knees. Tima stared back at the warehouse but saw no dark-light tentacles emerging from it. Her heart stopped trying to punch its own exit through her ribcage and settled down to a more normal level of hysteria.

'What was that? What *was* that?' she gasped, as soon as she could.

They both stared back at her, still gulping in air, shaking their heads.

'It's not coming after us,' said Matt eventually.

'How do you *know*?' asked Elena. In the dim light she still managed to look as white as a sheet.

'I just . . . I mean . . .' said Matt, suddenly dropping to his knees and then into a sitting position on the edge of the road. A little way along the kerb sat a bird—dark with a sharp, straight beak and oily-looking feathers. Matt nodded in its direction. 'She told me.'

Elena and Tima peered around Matt and stared at the bird. 'It's a starling, isn't it?' said Tima.

Matt nodded. 'Yeah—same as the ones that dumped their loads all over Dad.' He leaned towards the bird and laid his hand, palm up, right beside it on the kerb. The bird raised its wings, shuddered its feathers into position, and closed them again. Then it calmly stepped on to Matt's palm.

The horrors of the last few minutes at last began to recede as the girls watched him carefully lift the bird up and look it in the eye. The bird struggled to get a proper foothold, so Matt bunched his other hand into a fist and offered it. The bird hopped across, its fine dark-pink clawed feet gripping tightly.

'You did good,' Matt said, softly. 'Getting out of there. Your mates weren't so lucky.'

'*Lucky,*' the bird replied.

They all gasped and stared around at each other. 'It talks!' squeaked Elena.

'It mimics,' said Matt. 'Starlings are brilliant mimics. That's what you are, isn't it, Lucky?'

'Lucky,' said the bird.

'That's her name then, I guess,' said Elena. 'How do you know it's a she?'

'I just do,' said Matt.

'Can you control it, like Tima can control the moths?' Elena said, moving closer to Lucky, fascinated.

'Control isn't the right word,' said Matt. 'I know what you mean now, Tima,' he said. 'It's a . . . an agreement.'

Tima grinned and nodded. 'Yes—a kind of conversation. You can ask for something, and if they're OK with it, they'll help.' She glanced up at the lights, now dimmed again to the faintest orange glow by her moth squadrons. 'I don't think they'd do *anything* I asked. They'd weigh it up first. They have intelligence. It's rather . . . beautiful.'

Elena shivered and rubbed her arms briskly through her denim jacket. 'I'm hanging out with a *pair* of Doctor Dolittles!'

'I bet it's not just us,' said Tima. 'This has to be a side effect of that beam. You'll have it too.'

'Not so's I've noticed,' said Elena. 'But that's OK. I don't mind.'

Tima suspected Elena was the kind who made an art form of not minding. Something about the older girl was . . . resigned. Weighed down, almost. She really should find out more about these new friends of hers. She could work out why Matt was so angry, given what his father had done recently, but there was probably more to it than that. Elena, though, had not talked about her home life at all. Barely mentioned she even *had* parents. There was probably a reason.

'I think it's time to go,' said Elena, glancing back at the looming, silent warehouse. 'I know we haven't found out enough yet, but I don't think I'll ever be brave enough to go back in there. Whatever that thing is . . . that . . . demonic *squid* . . . I don't want to meet it again. We should leave it alone; let it go back to whatever freaky dimension it's come from.'

Matt stood up. Lucky stayed on his fist, flapping her wings a little for balance. He looked from Elena to Tima and back again. 'It might not be that easy,' he said.

Tima gently reached out and stroked the bird's wing. It glanced at her, untroubled. 'Is she telling you something?'

Matt nodded. 'Not in words . . . just . . . feelings. That thing—that *demonic squid*, did you call it? That's a good name. Whatever it is, it's hungry.'

'What can *we* do about it?' asked Elena, stepping further away from the building with a shudder. 'We're just kids. Should we be reporting it to somebody?'

'I don't know,' said Matt. 'We need to sleep on it. Well . . . as much as we can.'

They walked back to the perimeter. The industrial estate slowly brightened in their wake, as Tima brought the moth RAF off duty behind them. It was still reassuringly dim at the gate, though. Matt needed both hands for the ladder, so he paused and spoke to Lucky. 'Are you OK now?' he said, in a voice that Tima had never heard him use before—tender and gentle. The bird tilted its shiny black head and said: 'OK!'

Matt grinned and held his hand aloft. 'Fly home and be safe,' he said. 'I'll see you again, though, won't I?'

'OK!' cawed Lucky, and she rose from his fist. She flitted off into the darkness.

'That is . . . incredible,' murmured Elena. 'I wonder—' But what she wondered never came out. At this point she went rigid and then hissed: '*Listen!*'

At first Tima got nothing—but after a few seconds she heard it too. A sound like high-pitched, wheezy breathing—something straining with excitement. Then they saw the distant flash of a torch. Matt spun round and then gave a low cry of horror, pointing to the far side of the gate. Parked beneath the clump of holly trees they'd hidden under earlier was a small, dark blue van marked in white lettering: KNIGHTWOOD SECURITY—DOG PATROL.

'Oh my god!' yelped Elena. 'They've come round with an actual patrol! They HAVE!'

Matt ran to the rucksack, hauled out the ladder, and threw it up at desperate speed—but the sound it made seemed ten times louder than before. And the dog heard it too. They heard its thrilled bark. The man with the torch must have been right on the other side of the estate; his dog was clearly not on the lead. Its bark rang out in the night air, rebounding off the concrete and brick.

'Hurry, hurry! *Hurry!*' squeaked Tima, terror back in her throat. A low, dark figure was pelting towards them on four feet—it was seconds away. A cloud of insects swooped low in front of the beast. The Alsatian—clearly a dedicated working dog—snapped at the insects but did not break its speed.

'It's up! GO! GO!' cried Matt, and Tima shot up the rungs and then reached the spikes.

'There's no tyre!' she gasped. Matt gave a grunt of frustration and flung the tyre up so she could put it in place. The dog was maybe ten seconds from reaching them now. She threw herself over the tyre, across the gate, and landed on the concrete on the other side, jarring her knees painfully. Elena was up next, but it would be too late for Matt. The dog was nearly—no—the dog WAS there. Through the gaps in the gate, Tima saw it leap up and seize the boy by his arm and drag him to the ground. Matt gave a stifled cry of horror, his free arm flung up over his face. Elena was still on the ladder. Way off across the estate a man's voice hailed: 'Prince! Where are you, boy? What have you got?'

'No .. No, no, *no* . . .' wailed Elena, trapped on the ladder, unable to escape and unable to go back to help. 'Please . . . no . . . shhhh . . . no . . .'

Which was when the astounding thing happened. The dog simply let Matt go. It stopped snarling. It moved back on its graceful paws and stood still, silently gazing at Elena.

'We . . . we have to go,' whispered Elena. 'We're not here to cause any harm. We're not bad people.'

The dog stood still, tilted its head, and thumped its tail, once.

'Can you . . . can you help us?' asked Elena, in a low voice.

The tail thumped again. Another distant shout came from the security patrolman, but the dog did not respond to it, beyond a flick of its high, pointed ears.

'Please . . . please take your master somewhere else. Away from here. Away from us. Can you do that?'

The dog gave a small, throaty noise—almost conversational. Then it turned and ran full pelt back the way it had come.

The three of them remained a frozen tableau for five seconds, watching the dog head its master off in another direction. Then Matt leapt to his feet, grabbed the rucksack, and grunted: 'GO!'

CHAPTER 22

'Where did you go last night?'

Elena nearly choked on her cereal. She grabbed a gulp of lukewarm tea, playing for time. Eventually she had to say something. 'Blimey,' she said. 'Remind me that Cheerios aren't designed for inhaling! What did you say, Mum?'

Mum knotted her blue flannel dressing gown more tightly around her and took an unenthusiastic bite of her buttered toast. 'I said, "Where did you go last night?" I looked in on you at about 3.30 a.m. and your room was empty. I shouted down the stairs, but you didn't answer.'

Elena scanned her mother's face. How together was she today? Could she get away with telling her it was just a dream? Mum stared back at her; she looked quite sharp.

'I . . . well, I did nip out,' Elena confessed. 'Not for long. I

needed some paracetamol, and there was none in the house,'
she improvised. This much she knew was true. Mum had been
asking for some painkillers yesterday evening, but they were all
out of them. The headache had gone off after their evening meal
though, so Elena hadn't bothered to go and get some.

'You went out in the middle of the *night*?' said Mum,
suddenly looking horrified, like a normal mother. Elena nearly
cursed out loud. Clearly up until this point Mum *had* been
thinking it was more likely her meds, causing confusion.

'Yeah . . . I couldn't sleep anyway and my head started aching
and so I just got up and went down to the garage.' The garage in
the next road along had a 24-hour shop attached.

'Ellie—you can't just go walking around on your own in the
middle of the night!' said Mum. 'It's not safe!'

'Well, statistically speaking, it *is* quite safe,' said Elena.
'Studies show that 6 p.m. is the most dangerous time of day
to go out for a walk—evening rush hour; lots of accidents
involving pedestrians happen at the end of the working day. And
morning rush hour is the next most dangerous time. And then
it's between midnight and 2 a.m. in cities, because people roll
out of pubs and clubs and then try to drive home when they're
drunk. Most drunks—and axe murderers—tend to be snuggled
up in bed by half past two. Axe murderers just won't put the time
in after 2 a.m.; not enough victims about. So . . . going out just
after three was really very sensible.'

There was a pause during which Mum took another bite of
toast and seemed to zone out. Elena had her last spoonful of
Cheerios, her heart bouncing nervously, wondering if she'd got

away with it.

'Can you get me a couple of paracetamol then, love?' asked Mum.

Damn! Elena had no evidence. If only she *had* dropped in to the 24/7 garage and got some last night. 'Um . . . they didn't have any,' she said, getting up and clattering her empty dish and mug into the sink. 'I got ibuprofen . . . but you can't take those with quetiapine, can you?'

Mum shook her head. She didn't look suspicious. 'Don't worry,' she said. 'I probably just need another cup of tea.'

'I'll get some on the way home from school,' said Elena, swiping up her school bag and her cornet case. 'Or maybe you could have a little walk . . . go to the shops?'

Mum shook her head. 'Not today,' she said. 'Maybe tomorrow.'

As she closed the front gate Elena wondered whether her mother was getting agoraphobic. That was *all* they needed—a fear of open spaces to add to all her other fears. Global warming, flu pandemics, tsunamis—yes, even in the middle of East Anglia!—meteor strikes, the Tory government getting back in, rising house prices, *falling* house prices, the Tory government *not* getting back in, fracking, ash tree dieback, bee colony collapse, anthrax, too many immigrants, not *enough* immigrants. And these were just the ones she could remember off the top of her head as she walked to school. Oh—she'd nearly forgotten 'getting eaten alive by bears'. Ludicrous as it sounded, the possibility of this, after reading about some couple dying horribly in the Canadian wilderness, had stressed Mum out so badly over the winter that the doctors had upped her dosage.

One reason they had no Internet access at home, Elena had come to realize, was to stop Mum going online and torturing herself with an endless buffet selection of catastrophes that she or her daughter might encounter. Back when Mum had still gone online, Elena would sometimes come home from school to find her screwed up and motionless, like a dead spider in the corner of the sitting room, waiting for something awful to happen.

But she hadn't done that for a while. The meds seemed to be working, and she seemed more normal—if you could call a mother who was half zombie 'normal'. Sometimes Elena wondered if everything wouldn't be much better if she just stopped taking the pills.

And it might. For a while. Until the mania kicked in.

'Wait up!'

Elena jumped and looked around to see Matt catching up with her.

'How you doing?' he asked, puffing slightly. He'd been running.

Elena glanced around, aware of other kids now trooping along the road towards school. Elena Hickson and Matteus Wheeler walking together was bound to set tongues a-wagging. Then she decided, after what they'd seen last night, she didn't care.

'All right, actually,' she said. 'I think I got about two hours after I got back. How about you?'

He nodded. There was something different about him today; the sullen look wasn't in residence across his features. 'Yeah,' he said, falling into step with her. 'I reckon I got about two hours too. I'm ... OK.'

'So . . . what are we going to do next?' asked Elena. 'Do you really think that *thing* . . . that . . .'

'Demonic squid?' supplied Matt. He'd obviously taken to that name.

'Yeah, that. Do you think it's going to keep on coming?'

'Yes, I do,' said Matt. 'At least, Lucky does.' He glanced up, and Elena followed his glance. Above them, at telegraph-pole level, flew a shiny black bird.

'Wow! She's still with you?' She grinned up at the starling, filled with wonder.

'Came back with me last night, roosted on my windowsill,' said Matt, also grinning. 'I might have to buy some bird feed.'

'You're *not* taking her into school,' said Elena.

'Of *course* not. I'm not stupid. And neither is she. She's just keeping me company on the walk, and then I'll see her later.'

'Is that what she told you?' Elena watched Lucky flit above their heads, from one side of the road to the other.

'Kind of,' said Matt. 'It's not really words, is it?'

Elena finally allowed a glow of pride to rise inside her. Now she *knew*. It wasn't just Tima and Matt—*she* had the ability to communicate with animals too. The dog, last night. In their haste to get away from Quarry End they'd barely had time to talk about it. As the Alsatian ran off to distract its master, Matt had flown up the ladder, pulling the rucksack over his shoulder, while Elena had dropped to the other side. Then they'd worked the rope trick to pull the steps across after them, snagging the tyre down too, before grabbing the burglary gear and running as fast as they could away from the perimeter and the security patrol van. They were lucky there hadn't been another guard sitting in the van. After all this Tima just wanted to get home to bed right away, and Matt was bleeding where the dog's teeth had grazed his forearm. Elena had offered to clean it up and bandage it at her house, but he'd said no and just run on home once he'd dropped her off. Just as well, as it turned out, with Mum being so wakeful.

But the dog thing. Tired and freaked out as she was, the thrill of it hadn't left her. And this morning it was still making her skin tingle every time she thought about it.

'It's more a kind of . . . understanding,' she said. 'Matt?' She turned to look him full in the face. 'Is this *really* happening? I keep thinking it *can't* be real.'

He looked her squarely back. 'This is the most real thing that's ever happened to me.'

'GIRL-FRIE-END!'

Matt jumped and spun around to see Ahmed and Jed capering about on the other side of the road. He sighed. 'Here we go.'

Elena winced. Yes. This was going to be very aggravating. 'You could just get your starling buddies to peck them to death,' she suggested.

'I'll think about it,' he said, and took off to meet his mates.

She allowed herself to laugh. Yeah—school was still school—but there were bigger things to get uptight about. They'd already all agreed to meet again tonight to talk things through. None of them wanted to go back into the warehouse, but they couldn't just ignore what they'd seen . . . what they'd *felt*. They needed to think about what to do next.

School was uneventful. She was tired and quiet through her lessons, but being quiet was normal for Elena. None of her teachers noticed—even when she drifted off for ten minutes or so in Geography. On the way home she looked out for Matt but didn't see him. She dropped into the 24/7 to pick up paracetamol for Mum. The staff there knew her. She no longer needed to show them the small card that she took with her to the chemist when she needed to pick up Mum's meds. It said *Child Carer* on it, and gave an NHS phone number to call, to verify that she *was* allowed to take the meds away with her despite being only 13.

Elena didn't feel like a child. Or a carer. She just did her bit. She got the shopping and she cleaned and quite often cooked, but not all the time. On good days, Mum could do any of these things herself; it's just that you never knew for sure whether it would be a good day.

On a good day Mum would take care to stay off the news channels at dangerous times, and watch quiz shows and films and do crosswords and occasionally a bit of sewing. She had once been a costumier for a theatrical company and was excellent at dressmaking and tailoring. She'd been a freelancer and made decent money at it, but these days not so much. She couldn't guarantee to meet a deadline any more.

On a bad day she would forget her promise and watch the news and get drowned in fear. It might take a few hours—or days—to pull her back up to the surface.

So Elena was alarmed to find the TV showing a news channel when she got home. 'Mum!' she called, heading into the sitting room and going for the remote and hitting *mute*.

'I'm in the garden!' called back her mother, and instantly she relaxed. Mum sounded fine . . . and it looked as if this was just a short local bulletin, following on from some lifestyle show. Elena let out a relieved breath . . . and then sucked it in again as an image flashed up on the screen. A very familiar image.

It was Sentry SuperSacks . . . the warehouse. And it was surrounded by emergency vehicles. Blue and white police *Do Not Cross* tape twisted in the breeze behind a young male reporter as he addressed the camera. Elena fumbled with the remote and mashed her finger back on the *mute* button.

' . . . unexpected and shocking for staff who found the body here this morning,' said the reporter. 'A spokesman said the death is unexplained, and, although it may yet prove to have been natural causes, foul play has not been ruled out.'

Elena felt cold. Something had happened at the warehouse. Something very *bad*. And she knew what *bad* looked like. If they had lingered a few seconds longer last night, would it have happened to one of *them*?

She ran to dig her phone out of her school bag and immediately texted Tima:

Call me! NOW! Bad stuff at the warehouse on the news!

Damn! She *wished* Matt had got his phone back.

Her phone pinged and she eagerly read Tima's response:

Can't call. With Mum at hosp. Later.

She stood there, fizzing with anxiety and a mounting, terrible guilt. Someone had *died*. They should have warned people about that *thing*. The demonic squid. Whatever it was. Even if nobody had taken them seriously, someone might have kept people away from the fire escape door. They would have seen the dead birds again . . . they might have thought of a gas leak or something. She *should* have called the police!

Something shoved her, deep inside. She had to go. She had to *know*. 'Mum,' she called. 'I'm just going round Anne-Marie's place for a bit more practice.'

'OK,' Mum called back from the garden. Elena could see her on the sunlounger with a book. A sweet smell of warm, cut grass wafted in. 'When are you back?'

'In time to do tea!'

'I can do tea tonight,' called Mum, sounding really quite chirpy.

'Great—see you in a couple of hours!' bawled Elena, now at the front door. 'Byee.'

She paused long enough to stow her cornet case under the front hedge—she couldn't leave it behind if she was meant to be practising with Anne-Marie—but she didn't want to lug it along with her. Then she ran the whole way to Quarry End. It took her 15 minutes and, by the time she got there, she had a terrible stitch in her belly. She slowed down to catch her breath as she reached the open gates. Where was the security guy? How could she get in again? Say she'd forgotten to ask a question for her research? That was a bit thin, as excuses went. But as she walked closer she realized the security guy was deep in conversation with a van driver paused in the road. He was leaning in through the passenger window, talking animatedly.

So she just quietly walked past him. There was a fair bit of activity today—vans and trucks moving around the estate and a solitary police car stationed at the end of the turn-off that led to Sentry SuperSacks. Her heart pounded; should she go and speak to the driver; tell what she knew . . . ? If she did, she would have to admit she'd been inside the warehouse—and then try to explain *why*. And how *could* you explain all this to an adult, someone who lived in a world where moths *didn't* fly in formation when a ten-year-old girl asked them to, and starlings didn't talk, and guard dogs didn't respond to a polite request to be quiet and turn a blind eye.

She slowed down. Now what? What had she hoped to achieve by running all the way here?

'Are you OK, sweetheart?'

She started violently and then spun around to see a familiar face. It was Julie—the nice public relations woman who had shown her around Quarry End with Tima on Saturday.

'Oh—it's *you*,' said Julie. She was in a grey trouser suit today, and she looked rather more stressed than the last time they'd met. 'What have you come back for?'

'I . . . I just found out,' said Elena, waving towards the police car.

'Oh, you mean about Gary?' Julie stepped across and put a comforting hand on Elena's shoulder. 'Yes—what a shock! I've been dealing with the media all day. I suppose you must have seen the news on TV.'

'What happened?' asked Elena. 'I mean . . . we were just *in* that place on Saturday; I was so shocked when I heard about it. Was it the man we met . . . the one with the birds?'

Julie nodded, her face crumpling as if she might be about to cry. 'He was such a lovely man, too. Really friendly. Nobody knows what happened to him; people are saying heart attack or stroke or something, but he was a fit man—he looked after himself. And then there's the thing about his eyes . . .' she went on, staring towards the warehouse and continuing almost to herself. 'You're not telling *me* that's normal.'

'What . . . what about the eyes?' asked Elena. At any moment Julie was going to snap into grown-upness and abruptly stop telling her stuff. It happened all the time. But Julie went on, still staring at the warehouse. 'Jim Marshbury found him. We think Gary had gone in early to be ready for some new stock delivery; he was in before anyone else. His gate key was used just after 6 a.m. Jim was in at seven, and he found him all crumpled up at the back.'

'At the fire escape door?' asked Elena, forgetting herself.

'Yes, that's right,' said Julie. 'How do you know?'

'I don't . . . I mean . . . I just remember there was a fire door right at the back,' Elena said, hurriedly. 'What about his eyes?'

Julie shuddered. 'He was dead when Jim found him. Cold, too, like he'd been there all night, but he hadn't been. Security cameras showed him arriving about six, same as the gate key log. I got in as they were bringing him out on a stretcher, and the blanket slid off his face. His eyes were open and . . . weird.'

'Weird . . . how?' prompted Elena.

'Oh . . . I shouldn't be telling a nice young thing like you all this nasty stuff,' said Julie, abruptly sliding towards grown-upness.

'I'm not a nice young thing,' said Elena, quickly. 'What were his eyes like?'

'Like a pair of red buttons,' said Julie.

CHAPTER 23

Tima lay perfectly still while the world smashed and crashed around her. A week ago she might well have had a panic attack, stuck in the tight white metal tunnel of an MRI scanner with all its freaky noise, but not now. Truth was, she was fascinated. Would they find out anything about her brain? Was it different? Damaged in some way, even?

Having seen the beam, felt it and heard it, she was in no doubt how powerful it was. It had changed her—and Matt and Elena. Maybe a scan of her brain would actually show that up.

It was a perfect end to an already very weird day. At school she had glided through lessons in a kind of bubble. What had happened at the warehouse was so extreme that anything else was super-normal by comparison. She actually took great comfort from the super-normality. When, inevitably, Lily, Clara, and Keira had crossed the playground to greet her at the gates, she'd been ready for them. She even smiled when they started their patter.

'Oh, Tima . . . it's so *nice* to have you back!' said Lily, her face creased with fake concern. 'How *are* you?'

'Better,' said Tima. 'I encountered an evil, bird-killing squid-like entity in the back of a warehouse last night, but all things considered, I'm doing OK.'

Actually, she just stopped at 'Better.' Then she laughed out loud at the rest as it ran through her head.

'*Such* a shame you couldn't make the wrap party,' said Lily. *Wrap party? Did she think it was the end of a Spielberg movie shoot?!*

'Did your new agent come?' asked Tima, cheerily.

'She really wanted to,' said Lily. 'But she couldn't make it. I'm expecting to hear from her soon, though. She supplies child performers to the West End shows, and it looks like I will be ending up on her books. You have to have an agent, you know, to really get somewhere.' Clara and Keira nodded, sagely, as if they knew all about the business, right down to the contracts.

'Well, good for you,' said Tima. 'I'm pleased it worked out so well for you.'

'Yes—but I'm *so* pleased you're going to get another try,' went on Lily, linking her arm through Tima's as they headed into school. 'When Mr James phoned up yesterday and asked me to sing at the charity event the first thing I thought of was you. I said, "I would *love* to, but don't you think it would be better for Tima to do this?" I wanted to give you a chance to get past the trauma of just *choking so horribly* . . . in front of an audience of *three hundred*. I hope you're OK with that.'

Tima had nearly choked there and then, in front of an audience of three. Lily's lies were breathtaking.

'We thought she was right,' said Clara, taking Tima's other arm. 'You can do it! It doesn't matter if it's a bit wobbly, just as long as you get up there and give it another go. You have to deal with your demons!'

'That's the truth,' said Tima, fighting another surge of hysterical laughter.

All day, Lily & Co. had hung around, giving her their smug little pep talks. And all day she had smiled and thanked them and resisted the urge to punch each of them in the face.

So lying in a metal tube, assailed by a sound like a madman attacking the scanner with a road drill, was nothing really. Nothing at all.

'Nearly done now, Tima,' called the doctor, through her headphones. 'Thirty more seconds—just go on keeping beautifully still.'

At last the noise stopped, and the conveyor belt she was lying on slid her back out. Mum and Dad were waiting for her when she emerged into the lobby outside the MRI scanner room.

'You did brilliantly,' said Dad, ruffling her hair. 'And I bet your brain is perfect.'

The scan had happened very fast. Of course, it helped that Dad was a surgeon at this same private hospital. A perk of the job was getting your daughter seen within hours of a worried phone call.

'Can we have a look at it?' asked Tima.

'I'll check . . . see what they say,' said Dad, and he went into the room where the experts were studying her scans, without even knocking.

Mum squeezed her hand, but Tima could tell she was worried. This was *it* after all. The moment when they discovered whether their only daughter's head was messed up. Yet Tima felt pretty calm. She *knew* her head was messed up—but she was feeling better now than she had last week. She'd even got a couple of extra hours sleep after the scares of last night. If there *was* a tumour somewhere in her skull, it wasn't bothering her.

Dad put his head around the door. 'Come on in!' he said. He didn't look full of dread; in fact, he looked quite excited.

In the small room, which had a large window on to the scanner chamber, Dad and two white-coated experts were peering at images of her brain on a computer monitor. The walnut-shaped image shifted, shrank, and grew as a fair-haired woman in spectacles manipulated the mouse. ' . . . increased activation in the left-hemispheric angular gyrus,' she was saying.

'Look, Tima,' said Dad. 'This is really interesting!'

The woman—Doctor Wishart, according to her name badge—smiled at Tima. 'Come and sit next to me,' she said. 'I'll show you.' She worked the mouse again, and the walnut swirled and grew bigger. Parts of it were dark, and other parts now lit up in different colours. Two areas on either side were coloured in red. She could tell they were towards the back of her head, tucked just behind the ears, probably. 'These are what we call the angular gyri,' said Dr Wishart. 'They are in the language centres of the brain. They light up when there's electrical activity—communication stuff going on in your head.'

'OK,' said Tima.

'So . . . look at this one over here,' said the doctor, indicating a similar image on another monitor to her left. 'This is normal angular gyri from someone else's scan.' The image shifted, and white twinkles showed across it, like a sparkler on Bonfire Night.

'Now . . . look at *your* angular gyri.'

Tima's brain now animated on the other screen, and if the other brain had sparklers behind the ears, *hers* had an entire firework display. And if she wasn't mistaken, the red areas were both *bigger* than in the other brain.

'Is that good . . . or bad?' she asked.

'Well, we need to look more closely,' said the doctor, 'but as far as I can tell so far, it's neither. It's just fascinating. You have the biggest and most lively angular gyri I have ever seen! Studies have shown that this area of the temporal lobe is related to high language ability. So . . . you're probably really good at languages and communication.'

'I'm quite good,' said Tima, with a shrug. She didn't add that she could speak *moth*. And *bee*. And *grasshopper*.

'Has it always been like this, though?' asked Mum. 'Or does the brain sometimes change suddenly—out of nowhere?'

'Well, injury or illness can cause changes in the brain,' said the doctor, 'and that can sometimes affect a person's temperament and character. Some people even claim to have sudden new abilities after a knock on the head, but there's no reliable evidence to back that up. There's nothing here to worry about, as far as I can see.' She smiled reassuringly at them all.

Heading back across the hospital car park, past the

143

ornamental pond, Dad gave them both a hug. 'Stop worrying,' he said to Mum.

'Why is she worrying?' asked Tima. 'Because of the bees?'

Mum laughed. 'I'm not worrying any more,' she said, stroking Tima's hair. 'You *have* been behaving a bit oddly—but now I think it's just because you *are* odd. Just don't start cuddling spiders next, OK?'

Tima laughed too. *Not now,* she told the three dragonflies that were tailing her.

CHAPTER 24

How did you even *ask*? Elena frowned, glanced around the library to make sure nobody was watching her, and then typed: *Can anyone really speak to animals?*

The response to her internet search was, once again, a flood of nonsense. She picked through newspaper articles on so-called Pet Whisperers or Dog Psychics, loads of stories about cats and how they can read your mind, and some old legend stuff about animals talking at midnight on Christmas Eve. She sighed. This was going nowhere, and she didn't have much time—Mum was expecting her home for tea. She scrolled down the screen and flipped on a few pages, and then noticed a small link that read:

... some children could learn to speak the language of animals, if only their parents were brave ...

She clicked on the link and found herself on a website called PAGAN POWERS. The article was titled **'The Ancient Legend of Night Speakers'.** It read:

In pagan Britain it was firmly believed that some children could learn to speak the language of animals, if only their parents were brave enough to risk their child's life.

If a parent wished to give their child this power—which could lead to great importance and position in the community—they needed to take a huge chance and leave their infant alone and defenceless in a 'wild place' for seven nights in a row, following a full moon. Assuming the child was not devoured by wolves across this time, he or she would become a 'Night Speaker', instinctively able to speak and understand the language of all things. A Night Speaker would then have powers over the animal domain that no other human could possess, and could persuade a wolf, a fish, or even a fly to do their bidding.

The article ran on a couple more paragraphs, offering little more and no links to other information. To one side of it, though, was an image of a cave painting dating back to the Bronze Age. It showed a human figure kneeling among wolves and birds and fish, arms raised. The creatures were all positioned to suggest they were in rapt conversation with the human. Elena wouldn't have given it much more attention except for one thing. Across the top of the painting was a chalk line, bright and clear and as straight as a ruler, cutting just above the head of the kneeling human.

Elena felt the hairs rise up on her arms. Was she looking at the beam? The *same* beam?

Was she a Night Speaker?

Had the beam they'd all witnessed been active in their world for thousands of years?

She shook her head and closed the page down. It was time to go. The whole thing was stupid. If there had been a beam, creating messed-up kids like herself and Matt and Tima for centuries, surely the world would know by now. Night Speakers and their exploits would be all over the news.

And anyway, she was pretty sure Mum hadn't dumped her out in a field for seven nights in a row when she was a baby. Maybe she should ask, though . . .

As she left the library she nearly tripped over a small dog; a fluffy, flat-faced thing being towed along on a lead by a similarly flat-faced old lady. The pug growled at her, and the old woman eyed her suspiciously.

What's up with you? Elena asked, without speaking.

The pug stopped growling and sat down on the pavement, looking shocked. It glanced up at its mistress, who had doubled back and was tugging at its lead, and then back at Elena, with great intensity.

'He has a problem with his ear,' said Elena, suddenly.

The old woman stared at her. 'What?' she said, rather rudely.

'His ear . . . his right ear,' said Elena. 'I think it's an abscess or something; he's in a lot of pain and it's affecting his balance.'

The woman bent over and patted the pug's head—and the pug winced visibly. 'He *has* been walking a bit funny,' she muttered. 'Is the young lady right, Reggie? Does your ear hurt?'

Reggie whimpered and scuffed his front paw over the right side of his head. 'Well, I never . . .' said the old lady, glancing up at Elena. 'I think you're right. We'd better get that looked at. How did you know . . . ?'

'I—um—I'm studying to be a vet,' squeaked Elena, and she hurried away feeling hot and thrilled and freaked out all at once.

If she wasn't mistaken, she had just done a bit of night-speaking.

CHAPTER 25

In three years of stalking the shadows, this was the weirdest thing he'd ever seen.

For a start, what the hell were they doing out after midnight?

And for another thing . . . why the hell were they doing *that*?

He leant back against the Kowski Kar Klean wall and watched. Aside from insects, flying creatures were not so common in his nocturnal world—a few owls and plenty of bats, of course. But starlings? Never. He'd seen their murmurations on TV—great clouds of them in the sky, moving like a single entity at dusk. They would twist and turn in the air, creating impressive patterns for those watching below, but they were all roosting and out of sight long before *he* hit the streets.

So why were *these* thirty or forty starlings standing, beak to tail, in a perfectly straight line across the pavement and road? He shook his head, baffled. Over the past few nights his world had been changing: getting stranger by the minute, ever since he'd first spotted the fair-haired girl in the window of Jenkin Way. It wasn't the first time he'd seen someone look out of a window in the night, of course—but there was something about the way she had rested there, calm and contemplative, gazing out into the dark street with that faint Mona Lisa smile. He might have forgotten it if it hadn't happened again the next night . . . and the next.

He'd surprised himself by how much he wanted to talk to her, to find out why she was doing this. But the compulsion to freak her out was always going to be stronger, so one night last week he'd stepped out of the shadows. Singing *I'll spin you right round, baby, right round . . .* his black silk trench coat billowing in the summer breeze, he'd raised a hand to point at her, miming a gun. Just to see what she'd do.

Vanish; that's what. Her head jerked and immediately retreated into the dark of her room, and he, remembering what he was, had immediately retreated into the dark of the trees opposite. What had he been *expecting* her to do? Invite him in? She'd read the books and seen the films. She wasn't going to be that dumb.

Discovering the little posh girl on his beat was even more disquieting. On reflection (not that he really *did* reflection) he thought maybe chasing her had been a mistake. Uncool. She was too small to be prey. The boy—now *he* might be worthy of the chase. But so far just watching them all and wondering what the hell they were doing had been enough. The warehouse situation was the most unsettling. There was something very dark about that place—darker even than he. Something had happened; made them run, terrified.

It wasn't the dog.

It wasn't *him* either, which was quite annoying.

And now here were these ridiculous misplaced birds. Abruptly he stepped away from the wall and walked towards them, his supple black leather boots slapping quietly on the tarmac. The birds did not move. He was three paces from them and still they stayed put, although they glanced up at him uneasily. Only when he stepped up close enough to stamp on them did they flutter up and away around him, turning a spiral above his head and landing, one by one, along the guttering of the canopy over the car wash. He spun on the balls of his feet and raised his palms towards them. 'What?!' he snapped.

He could have sworn one of them said 'What?!' back at him, but at this point the twin flare of car headlights showed at the turn of the road, and he slid back into the shadows. The car passed and drove on out of sight.

He stepped back out in time to see the starlings swoop down and reassemble in the line. His watch showed 1 a.m. The half-Polish kid should be getting up soon, if he wasn't mistaken. OK. He'd wait. See what Car-wash Boy made of all this.

CHAPTER 26

Elena checked the pillbox. It was a long, shallow plastic tub, the size of a paperback book, divided into little square sections— seven across, three down—and marked from Monday to Sunday. Each day her mother took pills, morning, lunchtime, and evening, usually with her meals: lamotrigine at breakfast, lithium at lunch, and quetiapine at dinner. Monday's three compartments were all empty of pills. Good. That meant she should sleep well tonight, as usual. It was troubling that she'd woken up last night, but that was just a rare glitch.

Mum had certainly seemed deeply asleep as she peered into her room. Anyway, it didn't matter. She had to get out now, whatever the risk; had to talk to Matt about the death at the warehouse—and about the whole Night Speakers thing she'd found out, too. Tima had texted around 8 p.m.:

**Really sorry. Can't get out tonight. M & D checking in on me a lot
because of brain scan today.**

Elena had texted back:

What the?! R U OK? There's been a DEATH at the warehouse!

Tima's text came back swiftly:

**All fine. Tell you later. YES—saw news. We have to talk. Tomorrow
in the day maybe? Hve dance lesson after school. Cld bunk off.**

Elena had texted that she was going to see Matt, catching
him early rather than meeting him at 2 a.m. in the bandstand
as they'd planned. He was still phoneless, for all she knew. He
might have got it back by now, but she couldn't risk calling him
in case his dad picked up.

Keep me in the loop by text!
Tima had demanded.

Elena pulled on her green beret and denim jacket by the
front door. She laced her trainers tightly and then slipped
outside, pulling the door gently shut behind her. It was just after
1 a.m., and she thought she could reach the car wash in less than
twenty minutes. Maybe half that time if she ran. She glanced to
her left, at the soft orange glow to the east, and thought of the
creature reaching through the fire escape. She shivered, turned
away, and then broke into a run.

Her plan was twofold. She needed to talk to Matt about the death at the warehouse and the Night Speakers thing, and she also wanted to be outside his place by one thirty. Until last night she had never *seen* the beam. Now she wondered whether that golden stream of light was visible outside of the warehouse. Maybe the line she'd pencilled across the map actually showed up in reality for a few seconds in the night air, running from Matt's room, across the town to hers, and on to Tima's.

She reached Matt's road by twenty past one, having encountered nobody on the dark streets. She dropped to a walk, regaining her breath and calming herself. Matt wouldn't come outside for a good 15 minutes yet; she was too early. She should probably find somewhere shadowy where she could skulk, just in case a late-night motorist went by.

Then she saw the line. The straight line across the road. There was nothing golden or glowing about it, but it was a line, in exactly the place she had imagined it might be. It was shifting subtly in the weak glow of the street lights, and slightly glistening; it made her think of wet tar. As she approached she realized it was *birds*! Starlings! Her heart began to pick up speed again as she moved closer. The birds weren't flapping away. This must be Matt's flock of starlings: the ones who'd dumped all over his dad. *Wow!*

'Hey!' she murmured, her voice low and calm. 'Lucky? Are you there?'

One of the birds rose up higher and turned its head towards her.

'*Lucky?*' she breathed. 'Is that you?!'

The bird opened its yellow beak and said, 'Lucky?'

Elena went to kneel down near the feathery black line, hoping to make further contact—but a flash of distant car headlights halted her. She could not risk being seen. So she darted to the brick wall to one side of the car wash, aiming for the shadowy overhang beneath it.

And ran straight into a stranger.

Her first impression was a smell of grass and spice and then the sudden up-close warmth of another living thing. She let out a small cry of shock before the living thing grabbed her and slammed a cool hand across her mouth.

'I'd say don't scream, but it's such a cliché.'

The voice was low and lilting, amused.

Elena felt her eyes stretch wide. She froze, staring up into the face of a young man. He was dressed in black, with some kind of cowl around his head. His hair was white-blond, and his skin was luminously pale. Maybe a head taller than she was, he stared down at her with a fascinated grin. 'Seriously, though,' he went on, in that oh-so-light voice. 'Please *don't*. This will all work out so much better if you don't go off like a rusty klaxon the second I release that pretty mouth. If it helps,' he added, as she continued to stare up in mesmerized horror, snorting panicky breaths through her nostrils, 'I'm not going to bite.' The smile puckered at one corner, revealing a sharp white canine. 'Probably.'

Slowly he drew his hand away from her mouth, while the other kept a firm grip around her shoulder.

'What . . . what do you want?' she burbled.

'I'm really not sure,' he said. 'Does anyone *truly* know what they want . . . ?'

She shook her head, baffled.

'Oh I seeee—you mean, what do I want from *you*? Well, relax, Blue Eyes—nothing brutal. That's not my style and anyway, I didn't jump *you* . . . you jumped *me*. Here I was, quietly getting on with my business of sinister lurking, quite content and in no need of any help from passing ingénues. And all of a sudden—wham—you're in my face.' His voice lost its sweetness as he added: '*My space.*'

'I didn't see you,' she whispered. *Where was Matt? Would he be out yet? Was it time? She needed help here!*

'Are you sure about that?' he asked. The car had long since passed. He suddenly released her and stepped away, back into the pool of light beneath a street lamp. He turned, stood square on, and then lifted his right hand and pointed, as if aiming a gun at her.

'*You!*' she exclaimed. 'It was *you* staring up at me last week!'

He inclined his pale head and gave her a little mock salute. 'Nothing much gets past *you*, Mona Lisa,' he smirked. His face was lean and his eyes narrow. There was something other-worldly, almost translucent, about him. In the better light she could see he wasn't that much older than she was—maybe 15 or 16.

He could be in Year 11 for all she knew. The thought made her angry. 'Who *are* you? What do you think you're doing?'

'Who am *I*? What am *I* doing?' he echoed. 'What about *you* and your little friends, running around the town and breaking and entering into business premises? Messing with insects and birds. Strolling through my territory as if you own it.'

'You've been *spying* on us!' she said, with a short exhalation of shock. 'What for?!'

He suddenly moved towards her again, his long black coat flapping behind him. His eyes were something like turquoise—and gleaming with warning. She stood her ground as he brought his face close. 'I don't answer to *you*,' he whispered. 'And you're lucky I'm not in the mood to bite. Although that could change. At. Any. Moment. Your blood's so much sweeter than mine.'

She heard herself make a high choking noise, fear closing her throat. Then there was a growl. At first she thought *he* was growling, but then realized the sound came from behind her. She saw his face change: curiosity fighting with surprise and confusion.

'What new flavour of weird is *this*?!' he muttered.

There was a blur of amber, and the boy let out a yelping chuckle—half shocked, half amazed. A fox had shot out of the dark overhang and *attacked* him. It threw itself up, aiming for his face, but its jaws closed on his arm. The boy hissed at the creature and jerked the arm forcefully. The fox dropped but came again, this time going for his black-clad thigh with a whine of fury.

There was a sudden thud—a push of air and a smell like fireworks. A billowing cloud of smoke erupted in front of Elena's eyes, masking the boy instantly. The fox yelped. Several seconds later it was circling the road, staring around in bewilderment—and the boy was gone. Literally vanished.

Elena stood still, her hands across her mouth, shaking. She turned to look at the fox. It stood a few steps away from her, ears cocked and whiskers fanned, trying to scent its departing foe.

Then it turned to look back at her. She realized, with a rush of warmth, that it was the vixen she had met a few nights ago, on her way here.

'You *saved* me!' she said, kneeling on the pavement. The vixen trotted over to her. She remained still, watching. The creature came closer still, until it was eye to eye with Elena, and then . . . gently . . . it sat down and touched the tip of its black nose to hers. *Thank you!* sent Elena, from her mind. She did not expect the vixen to send back *'You're welcome'*, but she felt it all the same. A pulse of understanding. Much more than she'd felt with the guard dog. *Are we friends?* asked Elena, silently. The vixen tilted her head and dipped her snout. *Yes.*

How can this be happening?

It is happening.

But . . . how? Is it the beam?

The fox looked towards the line of starlings—which had suddenly formed again across the road—shuffling and preening, like a queue of mourners at a funeral. The fox looked back at her. In ordinary circumstances she guessed it would have taken advantage—seized a nice plump midnight snack for one of its cubs—but not now. It seemed to understand how important the line was. The beam. It got to its feet, glancing away, and she knew it wanted to get back to its young.

'Go—I'm OK,' she said, reaching out to touch the soft fur between its ears. 'But come back to me sometime, will you?'

The fox gave another little dip of its snout and then fled down the road, leapt lightly across a low brick wall, and vanished into an overgrown garden.

'What the hell is all *this*?' said Matt, stepping out from the car wash, gaping at the starlings. 'What are they doing? And . . . how come *you're* here?'

She got up and walked to him. 'They're marking out the beam. But that's *nothing*. There's been a death at the warehouse, I've been talking to a fox, and you just missed a vampire.'

CHAPTER 27

Tima lay awake, wishing Elena would respond to her text. It was a quarter to two. The beam had come and gone—and she was itching to get out and find her friends; to hear more about what could have happened at the warehouse to leave a man dead; to talk about what they were going to do next.

She'd heard the shocking news about Quarry End on the car radio as they'd travelled home from the hospital. Mum and Dad had been deep in conversation across the bulletin and quite oblivious to their daughter, frozen in horror, on the back seat. As soon as she'd got back from the hospital, she'd asked to use the computer and go online, saying she had school stuff to do. She did, as it happened, but that was the work of five minutes. As soon as it was done, she went in search of local news about the warehouseman who'd died in unusual circumstances.

There was scant information. He wasn't named, and there hadn't been any kind of autopsy at that point, so she couldn't really expect much more. But what Elena had texted yesterday evening, about his *eyes* . . . that was chilling. If they hadn't managed to get out last night, would *they* have been found in a heap with the dead birds? Would their eyes all look like scarlet buttons? It made her shiver to think about it.

She had planned to go out as usual, of course, but then her parents started talking about keeping a close eye on her, just making sure that all the MRI scan stuff didn't give her bad dreams. 'We'll look in on you, sweetheart,' said Mum. 'Keep your door open tonight, and we'll keep ours open, in case you need to call us.'

'Why would I need to call you?' she'd asked. 'I'm fine! The scan showed I'm fine!'

'I know, I know,' said Mum. 'Just humour me.'

And she realized that it was *Mum* who was still freaked and trying to get a handle on everything. Most likely she would just fall asleep and not actually check in on her daughter through the night . . . but Tima couldn't be sure of that, and if her night outings *were* discovered, she would never get out again. Ten-year-olds were not meant to be wandering the streets after dark. Even *she* wouldn't blame them for putting her on lockdown.

So she did the sensible thing and stayed put. But it was *killing* her. She'd woken up on the dot of 1.34 a.m. as usual, and now here she was, feeling like a party had started without her. She'd immediately texted Elena:

Where are you? What's happening?

161

So far, no reply.

She switched on her lamp and tried to read but just could not concentrate. She flung the book down with a huff and then went to the window, which was when she noticed the line. At first glance it looked like a telegraph cable, apart from the quivering and glistening of thousands of tiny, fragile wings. Fluttering and endlessly shifting, but still perfectly straight ... her moth squadron was hovering right outside the window, from the sill, and out across the road into the trees opposite in a ruler-straight line. A mime of the beam ... she was certain of it.

'What's up?' she asked, feeling her goosebumps prickle again (it was getting to be a habit these days). 'What are you telling me?'

The line drifted apart, and another shape began to evolve in the night air. Spinning out in curls that were first beautiful and then terrifying. They mimicked the exact writhing, darting movements of that dark-light thing in the warehouse last night. She gaped at it, transfixed, for nearly a minute before murmuring: 'I don't understand.' Then the pulsating curls drifted back into the straight line, shifting a little with the light breeze and a few spatters of rain.

'What are you trying to tell me?' she asked. 'That we have to go back there? Because I really don't want to!'

She did not get an answer because a taxi turned the corner of the road. The glare of its headlights and the unwelcome rumble of its engine scattered the insects. Then the rain began to fall in earnest. It was too heavy for her tiny friends to manage. She wouldn't risk asking them any more questions.

She got back into bed and texted the latest to Elena.

CHAPTER 28

'I didn't say anything,' said Matt. 'But I've felt like we were being followed, these last few nights.'

'Me too,' said Elena. 'But with everything *else* that's been going on, it wasn't top of my worry list.'

'It should be,' said Matt. 'What are you *thinking* of, running around in the dark on your own? It's just stupid. You're not doing it again. I'll meet you at your place next time, and then we'll both go to meet Tima at hers. She shouldn't go out alone, either. I don't care if we have to hide in her hedge.'

Elena bristled. 'I can take care of *myself*, thank you! I don't need a chaperone!'

'Yeah? And what if that fox hadn't shown up?' Matt realized how ridiculous he sounded even as the words came out. 'What was going to happen next? Some loser in a vampire outfit was just about to sink his teeth into you!'

'*One,*' said Elena, crisply. 'The fox *did* show up . . . and I think she will again, same as your starling friends and Tima's moths, if I need her. *Two*—he wasn't a loser in a vampire *outfit* . . . he . . .'

'Oh—you think he's a *real* vampire?!' Matt raised his arms up and let them collapse to his sides. '*Seriously?*'

'I'm not saying that,' she snapped. 'But . . . look, he was kind of *luminous*. And there was this billowing black smoke out of nowhere, and then he was gone.'

Matt opened his mouth to pour scorn on her—but paused. Hadn't Tima been talking about being chased by billowing black smoke when they'd first met her? He dropped his head, thinking, and finally asked: 'So . . . what *are* you saying?'

She shrugged and looked at the pavement where spatters of light rain were beginning to spread. 'I don't know—but if I'd told you two weeks ago that an invisible beam was going to give you the power to talk to birds, you'd have thought I was mad. Wouldn't you?'

He had to admit she had a point. If he could accept he was some kind of starling whisperer, that Tima could get favours from moths, and that they'd all been attacked by a demonic squid-like entity in a warehouse last night . . . how much harder was it to believe in vampires?

'Fair enough,' he said. 'But if you start doing martial arts moves and driving stakes into Dracula wannabes I'm taking *myself* to the nuthouse!'

'They're not nuthouses,' she muttered. 'They're hospitals.'

A moment later his skin prickled and he felt, rather than saw, the beam pass through. Elena gave a little gasp and blinked as that distant song echoed through them both. A moment later it was gone. 'Did you see anything?' he asked, but she shook her head. He turned to the birds, still holding their line in the middle of a shower of rain. He held out his left arm, fist bunched, and called: 'Lucky?'

At once a single starling rose above the rest and flapped across to him. She landed on his fist, fluttering her dark wings a little before finding her balance and settling. Matt felt a smile wash across his face—across his *soul*. This was something wonderful.

'We can see your line,' he said. 'Is that the way the beam goes?' Lucky gave a definite nod. 'So what's this all about?' Matt went on. 'What are you trying to tell me?'

Lucky gave a high-pitched rattle of bird call and then tilted her head, expectantly.

'I'm going to need more than that,' he said, stroking her wing feathers lightly with his free hand. 'Do you want us to go somewhere?'

Lucky lifted her beak and said: 'Go.'

Matt glanced at Elena. 'Go where? Back to the warehouse?' The bird twitched her feathers and flew off his fist and rejoined the birds in the line. There was a soft rustling of feathers as they rose up and flapped into the sky above the rooflines. More birds joined them from their roosts in nearby trees and began to move in that strange, hypnotic way he'd seen in the sky before, at dusk. The starlings twisted in a living cloud. He heard Elena draw in a sharp breath as it began to form twisting tentacles, stabbing and curling in the air. It sent chills across his skin.

'I don't like the look of this,' murmured Elena.

'Me neither,' said Matt. 'Lucky . . .' The bird flew back to his fist and fixed him with her stare. 'We don't understand what you want. We can't fight that thing.'

She took off and flew to the turn in the road, landing on a gatepost and looking back at them. The rest of the birds flew up and disappeared into the night.

'OK, then,' said Matt, with a shrug to Elena. 'I don't know what she wants, but we might as well follow.' They allowed themselves to be led, walking the dark streets as Lucky coaxed them on. As they walked, the rain eased off, and Elena told him about Gary, the warehouseman. He gulped hard when she talked about the red eyes. He could not forget the look of those two dead birds.

'This is getting serious,' said Elena. 'I think we might have to tell someone.'

Matt snorted. 'You mean you want to go to the police and report a funny singing noise and a beam that shows up once every 24 hours and evaporates in three seconds? Or did you want to make a statement about the demonic squid?'

She sighed heavily and then said: 'I know. I *know*. But I feel so guilty. We should have warned them.'

'Yeah, again . . . how?'

Elena shook her head. Changing the subject abruptly, she asked: 'How do you know Lucky's a she?'

'I just do,' he said. 'I looked it up at school today, though. You can tell by beak colour. In summer their beaks go yellow.

Blue at the base, though, if they're male, and pink at the base if they're female.'

'Wow,' she said with a chuckle. 'Matteus Wheeler ... looking up wildlife information! That's freakier than a vampire!'

'I'm not *stupid*,' he snapped.

'I know that,' she said. 'Um ... speaking of research ... have you ever heard of the Night Speakers?'

'What are they—a band?' he said, sullenly.

'No. I think *we* might be the Night Speakers,' said Elena. 'I found out something at the library today.' She went on to explain some ancient legend, involving kids being left out in the night and getting special animal communication powers. It sounded barmy. But didn't everything, these days?

'You think it's true?'

'I've no idea,' she said. 'But it has a nice ring to it: Night Speakers. I like it. We're out at night, and we speak to animals. It fits.'

It didn't take long to work out they were heading back to Quarry End. Their journey took them right back past Elena's place and then on to Tima's road. 'Oh!' said Elena, suddenly pulling her phone out of her jacket pocket. 'I told her I'd text. Oops ... she's got a bit cross!'

A list of increasingly agitated texts showed on her phone screen. She saw the most recent first:

Seriously! Are you even UP tonight? Have you gone to SLEEP?!

Elena spooled back up the stream of messages and then said,

'Whoa . . . look at this.' She showed Matt the phone, pointing to the second text:

Seriously freaked here! Moths have just been hovering in straight line outside my window!!! Then making scary demonic squid shapes!!!

Elena quickly texted back:

Look out window.

As they reached Tima's house they could make out her small face at a gap in the curtains. Elena and Matt waved and then walked on.

Aaaaaaaaargh! What's HAPPENING?!

demanded an angry vibration, three seconds later.

Starlings also in straight line!

wrote Elena.

Then demon squiddy. We're following Lucky. Will let u know stuff as soon as. B cool. Look out 4 vampires.

A barrage of vibrations followed as Tima desperately texted more questions.

'Leave it,' said Matt. 'We need to concentrate on what we're doing. She'll just have to wait.'

In the end Tima agreed to stop texting if Elena promised a full update in an hour.

They walked on quietly, watching Lucky flutter and swoop along the path ahead of them. As they got closer, Matt could sense Elena getting more tense. He felt the same. He really did *not* want to go back in that place. He wondered how he could explain that to a starling. Lucky had *been* there with them, though, when the weird dark-light started reaching its tentacles around the fire escape door. She must know what could be waiting for them.

'Maybe it won't be there this time,' said Elena, as they passed the town hall, all its windows dark and its cobbled car park empty.

Matt nodded. 'Yeah, maybe. It might only show up when the beam comes through. It's past 2 a.m. now. It should be long gone.'

'I hope so,' said Elena. 'But if so, how come that man— Gary—how come he was found dead there hours later? He didn't arrive until 6 a.m. according to Julie, the PR lady.'

Matt didn't have the answer. 'Look . . . you don't have to go in,' he said as they walked on past the power station. 'I'll go. You can wait outside and keep watch.'

'No way,' said Elena. 'You're not doing this on your own.'

He glanced across at her and saw that her chin was lifted and her jaw was set. There was to be no argument. Goody Two Shoes was brave, he had to admit.

169

When it came to it, their dread was unnecessary. There was no need to go inside the warehouse or even climb the gate— which was good news because Matt realized he'd left the ladder behind at the car wash. Lucky reached the clump of hollies opposite the gate and then, when they caught up with her, turned a tight arc in the air and flew to the chain-link fence. She did not cross it, but led them further along it, from post to post, towards the old quarry cliff face.

'O . . . K,' said Elena. 'That's the best news I've had all night!'

They ran after her, staying on the darker side of the little access road that followed the perimeter. They did not want to risk getting caught on any cameras. Without Tima there would be no moth squadron to cover them. And after last night's dog patrol incident, it was clear the area was getting more protection than they had thought. Lucky landed on the last concrete fence post, right up against the craggy, overgrown cliff face. When they reached the post she flew off along the cliff face, into the estate, staying more or less at head height. She landed on a small outcrop of chalky rock and peered back at them.

'Does she expect us to climb over?' asked Elena, eyeing the spikes along the top of the fence. 'You might need to get your steps and your tyre out again.'

But Matt was on his knees, rummaging around in the straggly shrubs and weeds that grew up against the fence. 'No need,' he said and pulled back a curtain of willowherb, shining his torch to reveal a large tear in the metal mesh, big enough to crawl through.

'How did Lucky know that was there?' marvelled Elena.

'She knows a lot of stuff,' said Matt. 'Come on.'

They scrambled through, snagging their clothes on some sharp bits of the ragged tear, and then began to make their way awkwardly along, wading through weeds and brambles that grew, in some places, to waist height. Lucky had led them to a kind of path that ran the length of Quarry End, skirting the cliff wall. It wasn't easy going, not least because there were other fences to manage. Two of the business units were fenced in at right angles to the cliff, cutting across this unofficial path. The first fence wasn't too high and had no spikes on top, so they were able to scale it and drop to the other side. The next one was higher and spiked. Matt pulled a pair of metal snips out of his backpack with a sigh.

'I'm officially a crim now,' he said, snipping determinedly and pushing either side of the wounded mesh apart so they could squeeze through. 'Breaking and entering.' He'd taken care to break through low down in a thicket of grass and weeds, so they could try to cover his handiwork with vegetation. When they'd crawled through they turned and pulled the greenery across the damaged fence as well as they could.

'You'd never see it if you weren't looking,' said Elena, pulling a leaf out of her hair.

The next fence was made of wooden panels. Easy. And not so easy. They jogged up to it and then drew to a halt, staring up at the dark overhang of some corrugated iron eaves.

'Oh no,' said Elena, with a shiver. 'We're here again.' They had arrived at the back of the Sentry SuperSacks warehouse.

Across the fence lay a darkness so thick, Matt felt he could almost touch it and feel its pulse.

'Is this where we need to go?' Matt asked Lucky, softly.

The bird perched on the fence and said, 'Go.'

'I forgot the ladder—I'll have to boost you over,' he told Elena. 'Then I'll take a run at it and vault.'

'Do we have to?' she whispered. 'What if . . . ?'

'If we don't go and find *it*,' said Matt, looking her straight in the eyes, 'it's going to come and find us.'

CHAPTER 29

'*Show me the way to go home*,' sang Elena. '*I'm tired and I wanna go to bed . . .*'

Matt gave her a look, but she didn't stop. She felt such dread that she had to sing, to make some noise that wasn't panicky inhalations or crashing heart or just . . . whimpering.

'*I had a little drink about an hour ago . . .*' she sang on, in a low, breathy voice, as they picked their way along the back of the warehouse to the other side of the fire escape door. '*And it's gone right to my head.*'

The flagstone path along the back of the building was carpeted with moss in some parts, thick with weeds in others. It was dank and cold and clearly nobody had been back here in years. There was another fence running, rather pointlessly, along the base of the cliff. As her torchlight fell on it, she could see it was rusty old chicken wire, kinked and drooping between metal stakes as high as her shoulder. It had probably been there since before the warehouse was even built, and most of it was engulfed in weeds. Except the bit right opposite the fire escape door. That was completely clear of weeds, revealing the naked white and grey chalk face just behind.

They both instinctively slowed to a halt. Matt set down his backpack, taking his torch from a side pocket. He glanced at Elena and then went to the fire escape door, which, on this side, was just a tall grey rectangle with no handle. She took a deep breath and followed him. At the foot of the door was a heap of dead things. Birds, bats, insects . . . even rats. She tried not to look at the eyes, but she couldn't help herself. She shone her torch down and sucked in her breath sharply. 'Matt . . .'

He nodded, grabbing her arm and giving it a squeeze. Dozens of red eyes stared up at them from the small pile of corpses, glimmering like hell's sequins.

'What are we doing here?' said Elena, unable to keep the fear out of her voice.

Lucky flew down and landed on Matt's shoulder.

'What now?' he asked. 'We're here. We don't want to be, but we are. So . . . what do we have to do?'

Lucky said: 'Do.' Then she flew across to the rusty old fence.

'Why are the weeds cleared away?' Elena pointed to the bare rock surface and the clear chicken wire. She reached out and touched the fence, and then both of them gasped as it disintegrated.

It simply turned to dust and dropped to the ground.

'Whoa . . .' said Matt, stepping back.

Elena coughed as a cloud of rusted iron particles billowed up from the collapse.

'It's like it was torched,' Matt said. 'All the weeds and stuff were burnt away first, and then all it took to finish off the fence was one little shove.'

Elena held her hand across her mouth and nose and hunkered down beside him to look at the dust. Something wasn't right. The dust had settled, but it was still, somehow, *moving* . . . in small tumbling waves towards their feet . . . and then retreating in the same weird pattern. Almost as if . . .

'Matt! There's something there!' she cried, dropping her torch in shock. 'It's like a draught of air, going in and out, like . . .'

'Breathing,' he finished for her. They both leapt to their feet and backed away, finding themselves flat against the fire escape door, as they stared down.

'Can you see it? Can you see any dark-light?' whispered Elena.

'No,' said Matt. 'It looks more . . . blue.'

And as they stared they began to see colour in the rock: a dim blue. And then they realized what they were looking at wasn't rock at all . . . but a hole in the rock, dark and blue-lit. It was about knee-high and a metre and a half wide with a curved top. A kind of low arch in the quarry cliff face.

Elena dropped to her hands and knees and began to crawl towards it.

'Wait—where are you going?' asked Matt.

'It's OK,' she said. 'The blue light is OK. Ask Lucky.'

Lucky, who had been perched on the remaining bit of fence, called out, 'OK.'

Elena crawled over the ashy remains of the fence and went straight under the low arch. Part of her mind was shrieking: *What are you doing?!* And another part was saying: *It's OK. It's blue.* It made no sense, but she *felt* as if the blue light meant they were safe . . . at least for now. She crawled on through, chunks of rock and loose stone digging into her palms and through the denim knees of her jeans.

'Are you really going in there?' Matt's voice, behind her, sounded hoarse.

'We're *both* going in,' she called back. 'This is what the starlings want us to do. And Tima's moths.'

'But . . . this is where the dark-light thing comes from, you do know that . . . ?'

'Yup. You want to turn back?' she called over her shoulder.

'No way!' he growled, as she'd known he would.

After a few metres of crawling, the low passage suddenly opened up into a full-blown cave. The cave was roughly oblong but not huge; you could probably just about squeeze a single-decker bus into it.

'Do you think the old quarry workers made this?' said Matt, crawling in and standing up beside her. He flashed his torch around, and it picked out rippling dark seams running through the pale chalk walls and ceiling. Underfoot was a carpet of ashy, crumbly stuff. Elena couldn't help but wonder if it was crushed bones.

'It doesn't look man-made,' She said, her voice slapping flatly back to her from the solid rock surfaces. She walked cautiously across the cave floor. 'Where's Lucky?'

'She's on my shoulder,' said Matt.

'Well, if she's in here too, we must be OK,' said Elena. 'I think we're meant to—'

Her words were snuffed out with the shock of the fall. One moment she had been on solid cave floor, and the next she was plummeting. She didn't even have a chance to scream before she hit another surface with a whump. Her torch spun away with a crack, and the light went out.

Lucky flew down after Elena as Matt yelled, 'Where are you?! What's happened?'

'It's OK—we're OK,' Elena called back. 'It's just a little way down. You can probably climb it if you're careful.'

Matt scrambled down over the lip of the upper cave floor and landed on his haunches, next to her. He put down his torch. There was no need for it; the space was gloomy, but he could pick out its shape with the help of the dim blue light. It was small—barely four metres across—and shaped like a bowl. In the centre of the bowl was another drop, this one no bigger than a manhole.

'We're not going there,' said Matt, pointing to the wisps threading up out of it. Wisps of dark-light. Elena grabbed Matt's hand and held it tight. He squeezed back, unembarrassed, and Lucky flew back to his shoulder.

'It comes from here, doesn't it?' whispered Elena. In an eerie echo, Lucky whispered back: '*It comes from here.*'

'Why are we here?' muttered Matt. 'What are we meant to do? If that thing decides to come up now, we're mincemeat. We can't stop it.'

'Stop it,' echoed Lucky.

'Well, yeah, we'd like to do that!' snapped Matt. 'But without superpowers I don't see how we can!'

'Can,' squawked Lucky. 'Can.'

'But *how*, Lucky?' breathed Elena, reaching out to stroke the bird's head. 'You need to somehow make us understand.'

Lucky didn't seem to have an answer, though, because she just lifted her wings and took off for the upper cave. Elena noticed something was different.

'Matt—the light—it's not so good,' she gulped.

The blue was reddening, turning purple. And now there was a low bass shudder, so deep it made her bones shake. The wisps of dark-light seemed to be making a claw-like shape. 'I think it might be time to go,' she whispered.

'No kidding!' Matt backed away from the dark-light well. The deep rumble now had a terrifying texture to it. Like the growl of an immense beast, waking up. They scrambled for the walls, seeking a foothold to get to the chamber above. But the walls were smooth, softened chalk and limestone like melted wax. They couldn't get a grip, slipping back down again and again.

Elena thought of the pitcher plants she'd once seen on a school trip to Kew Gardens—weird, smooth, tube-like flowers that enticed ants in, only to drown them in acid once they tried to escape. Their insides were too slippery to climb. Were she and Matt about to be drowned in dark-light? Glancing fearfully down she saw the claw was lengthening its fingers: stretching them out like hot toffee in twists of dark-light, ribboning through the air, seeking the prey.

'It's coming for us!' yelled Matt. 'How the hell do we get out of here?!'

'Here!' came the answer, echoing down from above, and the silhouette of Lucky moved to the far left of their slippery cavern. A dark seam was visible, running up through the smooth rock.

Leaping across one darting tentacle, Elena reached it first. It was barely wider than a ruler, but it was rougher than the surrounding rock—a seam of quartz. Elena grabbed for it with both hands and got a swift, inelegant boost from behind from Matt, who was yelling 'GO! GO! GO!' across a rumbling growl that seemed to vibrate her very organs. She was sprawling across the flat rock floor of the upper chamber seconds later, and Matt was up behind her, dragging her to her feet.

'Don't look back,' he bawled.

CHAPTER 30

Tima paced her room, staring at the clock. It was half past three now. Where were they? What was keeping them? Were they in the warehouse? Were they lying dead on a pile of birds and insects? She felt panic begin to creep up from her belly. She should do something . . . tell someone.

But *how*? It was just too bizarre. She couldn't imagine Mum or Dad believing it—and it would mean confessing to all the nights out with Matt and Elena. Then she really *would* be in lockdown.

She sent yet another text, begging for information. Nothing pinged back. Where *were* they?!

She screwed up her face and groaned. And then something snapped inside her, and she started to fling on her black clothes and jazz shoes. A minute later, looking every bit the cat burglar, she ran silently out across the large landing to her parents' room. Their door wasn't quite shut; she could hear gentle snoring. She peered around the edge. In the shadows Mum and Dad both looked and sounded deeply asleep. How likely was it that they'd get up now to check in on her?

To be on the safe side, she ran to the airing cupboard, pulled out three spare pillows, and then stuffed them under her duvet to look like a sleeping body. In a moment of inspiration she also grabbed an old doll from her cupboard and placed that on the pillow, covering all but the long dark hair on its plastic head. From her bedroom door, at a glance, it really did look like she was still in bed, snuggled down and sleeping, a few dark locks on the pillow.

Good. Now she crept downstairs with her small torch shoved into her black jeans pocket. She paused in the hall, thinking fast. Were one torch and a whole lot of attitude going to be enough if her friends really were in some kind of trouble at Quarry End? She considered for a moment. Turning back, she eyed the door to Mum's study. Dad's study was upstairs, full of medical books. Mum's was just off the hallway and also full of books and the stuff she needed to treat everything from a pet hamster to a shire horse.

Tima had one piece of equipment in mind. If she ever got found out they'd probably just give up and send her to a young offender institution.

CHAPTER 31

They tumbled back out into the open air, grazed and bruised by their flight through the low passage. The growl was still ringing in Matt's ears as he snatched up his burglar's rucksack and shoved Elena ahead of him through the cut in the fence. She didn't need much encouragement; she was already haring across to the next boundary while he crawled through, getting badly scratched, and stopped for three seconds to pull weeds across the damage to the fence. Madness. That dark-light thing could shoot across and grab him at any second. But he sensed that it wouldn't; that it had slowed down. Maybe it was too light out here now, so close to dawn.

Fear crashed through him, though, in huge buffeting waves. Fear like he'd never known, even when his dad was tanked up and at him with both fists.

They reached the final boundary and scrambled across the fence before dropping, exhausted, into the dewy grass underneath the trees on the far side of the perimeter access road. For a full minute neither of them spoke. They just breathed. Eventually Elena said: 'Where's Lucky?'

'Up there,' said Matt, nodding to the branches above them where Lucky was roosting. 'She really seems to think we can defeat that thing.' He rubbed his hands across his tired face.

Elena nodded. 'All we have to do is work out *how*.'

'I might know how,' said Matt, standing up and peering at the bloody scratches on his arms.

'Really?' Elena got up too and stared at him. She looked hopeful, like she really believed he could have the answer. He laughed drily. 'Come on. We need to get back. It's nearly dawn.'

'But you said—'

'I know what I said,' he muttered. 'I *might* know how. *Might*. Let me sleep on it.'

'Ha,' said Elena. 'Good one.' She held out her hand and called: 'Lucky. Come down. Try to tell me what you want us to do.' The bird landed on her wrist, preened, and stared up at her but didn't offer any suggestions. 'Do you mind, Matt?' she asked, as she carried the bird along.

'She doesn't belong to me,' he said, shrugging.

'No—but I think you belong to *her*,' said Elena. She looked at her watch. 'Oh no! I promised Tima I'd text *ages* ago! She's going to *kill* us for leaving her waiting so long. She—'

The words were knocked away. She was thrown sideways as something dark smashed into her. Matt gave a shout as he was shoved to the ground too. A moment later Lucky was flapping in the hands of a tall figure in a black cowl.

'So *this* is the amazing talking bird, is it?' The voice was light, conversational. 'Well now, I think I'll take this little wonder as a toll, for letting you cross my territory.'

Matt leapt to his feet and went for the boy but was instantly floored by a sharp kick to the chest. 'Seriously,' said the boy, holding Lucky firmly by the legs, despite her flapping and squawking, and lifting her aloft. 'Don't waste your time. I am trained to black-belt level, and I could kill you with one foot if I decided to. I could kill this *bird* with one *thumb*.'

'But can you dodge a bullet?' came a voice behind him.

And there was a metallic click that sounded very much like a gun.

CHAPTER 32

Tima thanked her theatrical training that her voice did not shake.

She held the pistol in both hands, pressed right against the base of his skull, and kept her voice steady and low.

'What you can feel is the business end of a Greener gun. It's loaded. Move . . . and it won't be.'

The boy froze. He did not try to turn around.

'Stay completely still, and keep your arms up in the air.' His hands, already held high with the seized starling, rose higher. His fingernails were long, pointed, and black, she noticed. He didn't speak.

'The Greener is very easy to use,' she went on, her belly like concrete, clamped tightly against the shakes that threatened to ruin this scene. 'It's for killing cattle or horses. Vets use them.

I know how easy it is to use, because I've fired it before. Don't think, for a moment, I won't fire it again.'

'I believe you,' he said.

'Now . . . release your hold on the bird,' she said, aware that Matt and Elena were staring at her as if she had just arrived from another planet. 'If you try anything, I might shoot you dead. Or I might just punch a hole in your spleen. I haven't decided.'

'I'm letting it go,' he said. He fanned out his fingers, and Lucky flew up into the night.

Matt held out his arm, and Lucky landed on it. He pulled the bird close under his chin, smoothing down her feathers and glaring murderously at her attacker. Elena was getting up from the ground, looking dazed.

'Good,' said Tima, easing the gun away from him. 'That's good. Now I want you—very slowly—to lie face down on the ground. Keep your arms outstretched. You reach for anything, I blast a window through you.'

He sank to his knees, arms still out, and then flopped forward on to his front, the long coat with its cowl hood billowing briefly. 'Isn't this a bit extreme?' he asked, his words slightly muffled by the damp grass. 'I was only *playing*.'

'Yeah,' said Tima, crouching down so she could bring the bell-shaped brass muzzle to within view of his dark eyes. In the growing dawn light they looked greeny-blue, like stones set into alabaster—his face was so pale. 'I know how you like to play. It was *you* who chased me last week, wasn't it?'

He didn't reply.

'And you who attacked Elena back at the car wash,' said Matt. 'You've been following us around. What do you want with us, you freak?!'

'Oh, don't flatter yourselves,' said their captive. 'I follow lots of people around. You aren't special.'

'Oh no?' said Elena, getting up and pointing two fingers down at him, pistol-shaped. 'How do you like the gun salute *now*?'

To her surprise he laughed. 'You got me there, Mona Lisa.'

Tima wasn't sure what to do next. Should they let him go? Tie him up and call the police? Erm . . . maybe not. As if he could read her mind he suddenly said: 'OK—so if you're going to shoot me, Princess, I think you should get on with it. It's getting late, and people will be waking up soon. Or did you all want to call the police? Is that the plan?'

They looked at each other, uneasily.

'I thought not,' he went on. 'So why don't we agree that I will just get up, go on my way, and leave you alone . . . and we'll forget this ever happened?'

'You don't get off that easy!' grunted Matt.

'Oh no? Well,' he twisted his head around to look up at Matt, 'whatever you've got planned, Car-wash Boy, do you think you might hurry it along? Only, the sun is coming up, and I don't do so well in the daylight.'

'You have *got* to be kidding me,' said Matt. 'Who do you think you are? Count Dracula? That is the lamest outfit I've ever seen, you loser.'

'Works for me,' the boy went on. 'Look, if we're going to

keep chatting, how about you introduce yourselves? It seems rude to keep using my pet names for you.'

'How about you tell us *yours*?' said Tima, with a little flick of the gun. She was beginning to wish they *could* just let him go. The gun was heavy, and keeping it steady was getting harder and harder. And the sun was breaking across the valley in wide pale shafts. They were all way too visible.

'Fine. My name is Spin.' He grunted and let out a breath. 'Nice . . . to meet you.'

'Spin?' said Elena. 'What kind of a name is *that*?'

'It's the . . . less boring half . . . of Crispin,' he said, breathing rather heavily.

'Oh . . . right,' she said.

'And . . . you?' he went on, screwing his face up and clenching his fists, arms still outstretched on the grass.

'Elena,' she said. Tima and Matt said nothing.

'Well, Elena . . .' He was shaking now. His voice was sounding increasingly strained. 'Perhaps you could ask your little friend here to lay off the local sheriff act now? Because . . .' he gave a groan and muttered, 'oh god . . . it's here.'

Tima, staring at his face across the increasingly trembly gun, noticed something weird in the dawn light. That pale, almost translucent skin was reddening in patches. The blotchy wash of colour moved fast, from his jaw up to his brow.

'Stand away,' he groaned. 'I'm not going to . . . oh god . . . just get away from me, all of you.'

Alarmed, she stepped back, still holding the gun but barely aware of it now as she watched him get to his feet. His hands . . .

his hands were reddening too . . . in vein-like shapes.

Elena and Matt had moved backwards as well, Matt still clutching Lucky tightly to his chest. But Spin—or whoever he was—no longer seemed to care about Lucky, or about any of them. He gave a hoarse cry and pulled the black cowl up over his head and down across his face. Then he turned and fled into the trees just as daybreak washed them all gold.

CHAPTER 33

'Where did you get *that*?!' Matt took the gun out of Tima's shaking, sweaty hand. 'Is it loaded?' She nodded, still staring into the trees where Spin had vanished.

Elena gave her a hug. 'That was amazing!' she said.

'Where did you get this?' asked Matt, again.

Tima shrugged. 'From my mum's study. She's a vet. Sometimes she has to put down horses or cattle, and this is what she uses. It's the Greener Safti Cattle Killer. An antique but it still works. She will go absolutely nuclear if she ever finds out I borrowed it.'

'It looks like some kind of Wild West pistol,' observed Matt, turning the heavy brown metal gun in his hands.

'You wouldn't really have shot him, would you?' asked Elena.

Tima took the gun back from Matt with shaking hands. The

last few minutes had taught her just how terrifying an object it was. What if it had gone off? What if that boy had ended up bleeding on the pavement? Dying? She took a deep breath. 'No. I was bringing it with me for scarier things than *him*.' She emptied its chamber and put bullets and gun into her jeans pockets. 'I thought you'd both gone back to the warehouse and been attacked by the Squid Demon of Dark-light! Why didn't you text me?!'

'I was just about to,' said Elena. 'We haven't been into the warehouse. We've been somewhere even freakier.'

They walked Tima back home, filling her in on the events of the past few hours. She listened, fascinated and horrified. 'It nearly had you!' she murmured. 'What were you thinking of?'

'So you *wouldn't* have gone in there?' challenged Matt.

'Well . . . maybe,' she admitted. 'But what do we do now? How are we meant to fight this thing?'

'Matt's got an idea,' said Elena.

Matt whispered something to Lucky and then sent her up into the dawn sky where she circled once and then flew west. 'I don't want to talk about it yet,' he said. 'It might be stupid. I'm too tired to know.'

Tima rolled her eyes. 'Caves. Dark-light. Bird-snatching vampires. Guns . . .' she said. 'My freakometer is going to break.'

They reached Tima's road. 'Right,' said Matt. 'I don't want to sound like my old man, but we need to get some sleep. Good sleep. There's not much time left now.' He sighed, looking at his watch. 'I'll be cleaning cars in an hour. We need to make a plan when we've had some rest and can think straight. Elena and I can talk on the way to school—and Elena will have to text you, Tima.'

Tima and Elena nodded. Tima glanced anxiously at her house as they neared it. 'I hope Mum and Dad are still asleep. These fun times could be over if they're not.' She turned suddenly and pulled them all into a group hug. 'See you tomorrow—in the night again, yeah? If Mum and Dad don't find me out for *this* little outing.'

'I think we should meet earlier if we can,' said Matt, disengaging himself awkwardly. 'Half past twelve, maybe. But wait for us here. You're not going anywhere on your own. That stupid vampire kid might be about.'

'Did you see his skin?' asked Tima.

'He uses white make-up, I bet,' said Matt, with disdain, adding a list of colourful names for his attacker.

'No,' said Tima. 'I mean later, when the sun came up. Didn't you see? His face and hands turned red. That's why he was making that noise. I think he was in pain.'

Elena and Matt stared at her for a few seconds. Then Matt gave a harsh laugh. 'Don't tell me you seriously think he *is* a vampire!'

'I'm not telling you anything,' said Tima. 'Just what I saw.'

'And there *was* the smoke thing,' added Elena. Matt shot her a contemptuous look, and she raised her hands. 'I'm just saying!'

'He's a faker,' said Matt. 'But he could still be dangerous. So I'll meet Elena first, and then we'll come to you. We'll wait here by the hedge, OK? We won't be seen from your house.'

'OK,' said Tima. She watched them go and then crept

back into the house, fear mounting with every creak and thud she caused. She went back into Mum's study to put the gun back, breaking into a cold sweat of fear when the desk drawer rasped and clunked. She closed it as quietly as she could and then crept back upstairs to her room. The pillows and the doll were undisturbed. Even in the brightening light it was quite convincing. She took the spare pillows back to the airing cupboard, chucked the doll under her bed, undressed, and crept under the duvet. The shakes she'd held in earlier suddenly rattled through her body. Had she really planned to fire a gun? She didn't even know *how*!

It was after five now. It was possible she could get two hours' sleep, maybe. She was just beginning to drift off, when there was a click and her door was pushed open. Through half-closed lids she saw her mother quietly pad across the carpet and smile down at her. She faked sleep, and Mum wandered back to her own bed a few seconds later.

She'd got away with it.

This time.

CHAPTER 34

Matt had never had a pet. He'd *wanted* one, of course. A dog. A cat. A hamster. Even a goldfish would have done. Dad, though, thought they were a waste of time and money. Every plea from his son fell on deaf ears. The closest they'd ever come to animal company was when a family of rats had set up house under some old boxes at the back of the car wash. The baby ones were so cheeky, running along the back wall, whiskers twitching. He had thrown some crisps to them once and watched in delight as three of them each grabbed one in their furry mouths and hurried away back to the old boxes.

Dad had poisoned them all a week later.

So having Lucky was almost dreamlike for him. She was on his windowsill when he woke up from the 45 minutes of sleep he managed to get. She sat companionably on top of the jet wash machine as he soaped a Nissan Micra, and whenever Dad wasn't around they chatted. Kind of.

She never said much. Maybe all she ever did was mimic him. Yet there was always a kind of logic to her responses.

'Do you know what the beam is?' he asked.

'No,' she said. Or it could have been 'Know'—it was impossible to tell.

'Do you think my plan will work?'

'Work.'

She went with him to school, flying from telegraph pole to street lamp to bus shelter, always landing and looking back for him. He seemed to have missed Elena—he'd have to find her at lunchtime or after school—but having Lucky for company was more than enough. As he neared the school gates he had to call up to her, softly. 'Don't come in with me. I'll see you afterwards.' He couldn't risk her landing on his shoulder when his mates were around. They could be such idiots; one of them might chuck something at her or try to grab her.

She seemed to understand and flew away.

He was told off twice in class for drifting. He wasn't exactly asleep, but the tiredness was heavy on him, making him slow and dopey in his responses. At lunchtime he was hanging out with his mates when Elena walked by, carrying her cornet in its little black and silver case. He had to stop himself smiling back at her when she smiled at him.

'Look—it's your girlfriend!' whooped Ahmed, and the others all joined in like a bunch of baboons, name-calling, leaping up and down, making rude gestures. Not long ago he would have found it funny. Now it was just incredibly irritating. He told them to shut up—in words they understood. They stared at him, grins fading, glancing at each other.

'Man . . . you is well out of order,' said Ahmed in that gangsta slang he pretended was real. Matt knew he actually lived in a nice house with a middle class family and had no idea what half the slang he used even *meant*.

Matt didn't bother to respond. He just jumped off the brick wall they'd been lounging on and went back into the school building, taking care to go in the opposite direction from Elena. She'd had the sense not to stop and talk—or look back when the catcalling started. The whole 'girlfriend' thing really grated on him because Elena was *more* than that. She wasn't one of those giggly, flirty types, trying to get attention. She was *real*. She was a friend. Elena and Tima, he realized, with a slight rush of shock, were the most important friends in his life.

He drove his hands into his pockets and ambled along the corridor, head low, wondering where to go. Then he astonished himself by climbing the stairs to the library. The librarian did not look welcoming. He'd been in there too many times with his mates just to eat crisps and mess around, annoying other kids who liked reading. The librarian's look of wariness changed to mild confusion when he asked about a book.

'Come this way,' she said, as if she'd just got the *best* birthday present ever.

Elena's band practice went well. Despite having slept for only about three hours, she managed to hit all the notes in the right order and on time. Mr Gould was clearly very relieved that she'd managed it without any hysterical weeping. They were performing three tunes at the charity event at the town hall that Wednesday evening. In her new world of darkness, demons, and vampires, the simple playing of her cornet was very reassuring. She had a short solo of Grieg's 'Solveig's Song' to perform: a lilting tune that rang out of her instrument with sad intensity.

It was hard to imagine performing it on Wednesday. This was Tuesday, and the concert was only a day and a half away, but who knew where she would be by then? There was a dark-light demon to sort out, and she hadn't a clue how they were going to do it.

When they were finished and putting their instruments away, she went over to Anne-Marie, her clarinettist friend. Anne-Marie was in Year 11, over on the sixth-form campus, and sometimes they practised round her house after school. 'Anne-Marie—do you know a boy in your year called Spin?' she asked.

'Spin?' echoed Anne-Marie, fiddling with her reed. 'What kind of name is that?'

'The less boring end of Crispin,' Elena said.

Anne-Marie shook her head. 'Don't know any boy called Spin *or* Crispin. Why?'

'Ah—nothing,' said Elena. She hadn't expected anything else really. She went up to the library for the last ten minutes of her lunch hour and saw Matt there, reading a book.

'Now *my* freakometer's broken,' she murmured.

He looked up and gestured her over. 'I spoke to the librarian. I asked about . . . the underworld.' He looked a little embarrassed as he showed her an old leather-bound book, open at an inky picture of a glowing cave with malevolent eyes peering through some kind of drifting mist or smoke. Elena sat down next to him, dumping her bag and cornet case at her feet. 'There are *loads* of underworld demons and gods,' he went on, quietly. 'But the demon thing is just loads of religious stuff and nothing that looks or sounds like our . . . thing. I was going to call it the DLD—for Dark-Light Demon . . . but now I'm thinking DLG. Dark-Light *God*.'

'DLG,' said Elena. 'Why *god*?'

'Because there's a *shedload* of gods. I thought they'd be, you know, Greek or Roman or something—but they're right here in *England*! I mean, all over the *world* too, but *here*—in *England*? I never knew.'

'Seriously?' said Elena. 'I've never heard of any.'

'Me neither, but look—there's a whole freakin' alphabet of them!' He flipped over to a page with a long list of names. 'There are only a few underworld ones I've found so far, though. Most are gods of mountains and rivers and stuff. Arawn, though, is from the underworld kingdom of the dead,' he whispered, running a finger down the entry.

'Revenge, terror, war,' read Elena. 'Could be our guy then.' She wasn't sure how seriously she could take this.

'Nah,' said Matt. 'He's in Wales.'

'I expect they can travel,' she said.

'Then there's Black Annis in Leicestershire,' Matt continued. 'Blue-faced hag underworld thing; eats kids. Sounds like a fairy story, though, that one.'

'Don't they all?'

Matt looked up at her, narrowing his eyes. 'Are you taking the—'

'Perhaps there's one that looks like a demonic squid,' said Elena. 'Which also, now I come to say it out loud, sounds like a fairy tale.'

'Yeah,' he said, coldly, going to close the book.

'Sorry,' she said, stopping him and pressing it open again. 'This is good research. And *I* didn't think of it. Go on. Who else have you got?'

'Only one other English underworld god,' Matt said, glancing around to check they weren't being watched. 'Arimanius. Head of a lion, apparently.'

Elena weighed this up. 'Could be,' she said. 'There *was* a lot of roaring last night. Does it really make any difference? Whatever it is; whatever name it goes by—we just have to keep it in its own world. Under. Not over.'

Matt flipped over some more pages and read aloud, in a hushed voice, from a dense block of text. '*Some druids believe that ancient deities are merely sleeping, and a disturbance in the human realm can wake them. That disturbance can be anything from a violent storm to aggressive building or demolition work or strong electrical fields. Misdirected electrical energy in particular can thin the walls between the overworld and underworld.*'

'The beam,' breathed Elena.

'The beam,' agreed Matt. 'It feels electric, doesn't it? Well, it makes *my* hair stand on end, anyway. So every time it comes through, I reckon it's whipping up this Dark-Light God or whatever it is. (I'm calling it the DLG for short, now.) Making it rise up into our world and mess with any living thing it finds. Birds, insects, animals . . . the warehouse guy.'

'And the beam keeps coming,' said Elena. 'And the Dark-Light God is getting bolder every time. Travelling further. Staying up longer.'

'And we don't know how to stop the beam,' said Matt. 'So we have to do the next best thing. We have to seal off the DLG's den so it can't feel or hear the beam any more. Or can't get through even if it does.'

'How do we do that?'

Matt grinned, closing the book. 'I've got a plan.'

CHAPTER 35

Tima should have been dead on her feet. She'd had about four hours' sleep, tops—and this time last week she could barely function on that. But today, strangely, she was OK.

She went through the dance routine with Lily and the others for 'Consider Yourself'. It was a great rehearsal: cheery and fun (as long as she paid no attention to the whispering and sniggering). Ryan Brent, who played Dodger, grinned and gave her a high five at the end of it. 'Cool that you're back, T,' he said. 'Don't freak out again, yeah?'

She grinned back at him and said: 'No freaking out this time.' And she felt pretty confident about that. After everything she'd dealt with since her last onstage experience, getting up in front of a hall full of people for a song-and-dance routine was *nothing* she couldn't handle.

Her new confidence rang out in her voice and spun out with her dance steps. She felt as if she was glowing—powerful and different. She could communicate with the insect world and persuade it to help her! She could hold a gun to the head of someone who might very well be undead! What was a little school show?

Mr James finished his last piano flourish at the end of her solo and spun around on his seat, face lit up. 'Tima, that was the best you've ever done it! You'll make us all proud tomorrow night.'

She beamed back at him, dipped her head, and said: 'Thank you.'

It would have been a golden moment if she hadn't spotted the sour look on Lily's face.

'Lily, Ryan, Joe, and Archie—you were fantastic too,' added Mr James, but Tima knew it was too little, too late.

'Aren't *you* the special one?' muttered Lily as she swept past. 'Let's hope you can hold it together this time and not mess up, eh?'

Tima decided the best thing was to pretend she hadn't heard. There wasn't much she could do about Lily. Trying to be nice to her would only make her *more* superior. The rehearsal had ended, and as they filed out of the school hall she held back, leaving as much space between herself and Lily as she could.

Mr James, clutching his folio of sheet music, caught up with her. 'The mayor is going to be at the charity show,' he said. 'Don't be overwhelmed, though—she's just a nice lady wearing a big golden chain. If you just do what you did this afternoon, you'll be fine. Are your mum and dad coming?'

'Yes,' said Tima. 'They wouldn't miss it—not after missing the school show, because of . . . you know.'

'Did your doctor get to the bottom of that?' he asked.

'Kind of. They think it was just a kind of exhaustion thing. I'm fine now.'

'Good,' he said. 'Because . . .' he stopped and turned to look at her, concern in his eyes, ' . . . you seem a bit, well, *wired,* if you know what I mean. Quite . . . buzzy.'

'It's OK,' she said. 'I'm just excited.'

'Good. Excited is good—but perhaps you should take a few long, deep breaths every so often. Calm yourself right down. Meditate, even. That should help balance things out and stop you getting overhyped and exhausted. There are some great books on mindfulness in the library. Have a look.'

'I will,' she said, and he nodded and went on his way.

She took deep, slow breaths all along the corridor, even when she passed Lily, Clara, and Keira and heard Lily say:

' . . . unstable. I bet she'll freeze again. Mrs Theroux has asked me to be on standby to take over, just in case.'

Now *there* was something to be mindful about.

CHAPTER 36

Spin lay still. Sometimes, if he kept completely still, he could pretend the pain had gone.

Enveloped in darkness, he tried not to think about what had happened, because every time his thoughts went back to that ignominious encounter with a *ten-year-old* packing a gun, his nerves prickled and crackled, and it felt like someone was flicking a blowtorch across his skin.

It will pass. It will go, he told himself, again and again. The sun had only found him for a minute or two. He had survived worse than this.

Just what was going on with them and that industrial estate? He longed to know. He hoped he would recover in time to be out again tonight. He wanted to stalk them again, closer this time, and listen in; find out what they were up to. It had something to do with that warehouse, the cliff behind it, and the bird, the fox, and the insects. It was a baffling—intriguing—puzzle. If he felt up to it, he could break into the warehouse tonight, earlier, before they usually came out. Have a scout around. Before then he needed to do a little research: see if there was anything in the old books about this peculiar set of circumstances. Find out what measures he needed to take.

Then he needed to think of a way to get them all cornered. The balance of power had shifted when Little Miss Princess had trained that gun on him. This needed to be redressed. He could *not* leave them all with the upper hand. He would corner them and pin them and make them give up their secrets.

An excited fizz bloomed through him; this was a worthy game. He didn't know how it would end, but the blood rush was upon him.

Even as he thought this, his own blood blackened and burned, and he groaned aloud with pain.

CHAPTER 37

'Our brains are different,' said Tima.

'How so?' asked Elena, with a stab of fear. What had Tima's MRI scan shown up?

'The language centres in mine were way bigger than normal and going off like fireworks on New Year's Eve. I could see it all on the screen when they replayed my scan video. Yours will be the same. And Matt's. I'm sure of it.'

Elena pressed her hands to the area just behind her ears that Tima was indicating. 'So—our brains have kind of ... mutated?'

'I prefer "evolved",' said Tima.

'And now we're Night Speakers,' said Elena.

'It does sound kind of cool,' said Tima. She'd been brought up to speed on the things Elena and Matt had discovered in libraries over the past couple of days. 'But it doesn't mean we can defeat this DLG, does it? What is Matt's plan?'

'I'm not sure—but here he is now,' said Elena as Matt jumped over the low wall and ran towards the bandstand. 'We're about to find out.' In the distance the town hall clock was chiming twelve. Matt had told her that afternoon that she'd have to meet Tima on her own after all, and he would join them slightly later.

'What are you two looking so worried about?' he said as he leapt up the steps and into the bandstand. 'Wannabe vampire boy show up again?'

'Not if he knows what's good for him,' growled Tima.

'Did you bring the gun?' asked Elena.

Tima shook her head. 'No. I don't think Spin or whatever he calls himself will bother us again.'

'Too right,' sniggered Matt. 'He'll be back in his coffin for a week after the sun burnt him up.'

Tima exchanged glances with Elena, and Matt didn't miss it. 'Seriously, you two? You really think he's an *actual* vampire?' He shook his head in disgust. 'You should have brought a wooden stake then.'

'Tell him about your brain,' said Elena.

'It's not just me,' said Tima. 'It'll be both of you too. The MRI scan showed up something freaky,' she explained to Matt. 'The language and communication bits in both lobes of my brain are bigger and more active than anyone else's they've ever seen. The beam—travelling through our rooms—right through our *heads* for all we know; it's changed our brains. That must be how we can communicate with animals.'

'Is it dangerous?' asked Elena.

Tima shrugged. 'They don't think so. But I've got to have another check-up in six months.'

'Why did your parents even take you for a scan?' asked Matt.

'Hmm,' said Tima, 'That'll be the bee beard thing.'

'Parents, eh?' Elena rolled her eyes. 'One *little* bee beard and they freak.'

Matt shook his head. 'If *I'd* seen you do that I'd have had you carted off to the funny farm.'

'They're not *funny farms*,' snapped Elena.

Matt stared at her. Then he shrugged and said: 'OK, brain freaks. In the truck.'

'Erm . . . what?' said Tima.

'Come on.' Matt jumped down off the bandstand and led them back to the road. Parked deep under the trees at the side of the residents' gardens was a grimy white flatbed truck. A blue tarpaulin was tied over something lumpy in the back.

'What the—' began Elena.

'Yup,' said Matt.

'But—you're underage! You haven't got a licence!' squeaked Tima. 'Do you even *know* how to drive?'

'I've been moving cars around the car wash forecourt since I was 12,' said Matt. 'It's not illegal to drive on private land without a licence.'

'But it IS illegal to drive on roads,' pointed out Elena.

'Look,' said Matt. 'How many police cars have you seen since we've been coming out nights? None. And anyway, if one did drive by, three kids dragging sacks of rubble along the pavement is going to look a lot more suspicious than a passing car!'

'We've got sacks of rubble?' Tima queried.

'And some scrap metal,' said Matt, with a grin.

Elena stared at him for a moment and then nodded. 'I get it,' she said. She thought she knew what Matt's plan was now. She wasn't sure it would *work*, but it was worth a try.

Matt's driving wasn't smooth. His gear changes jolted, but he seemed to know what he was doing. Tima, belted in along the passenger bench seat next to Elena, raised her eyebrows, impressed. 'Whose truck is this?'

'Dunno,' said Matt. 'Someone dropped it in for a valet last night. I'll be cleaning it up first thing tomorrow.'

'And whose rubble?' asked Elena.

'Found it in a skip down the road. Nobody wants it. It's not stealing.'

'So—this well into the underworld,' said Tima. She paused and shook her head. 'I still can't believe this is really happening. Anyway . . . you think this is where the dark-light god . . . your "DLG" is coming from?'

'We don't think. We know,' said Matt, changing down a gear and rattling the truck around a tight bend past the town hall.

'And the plan is to block it up? With rocks?'

'Yup.'

'The hole isn't that big,' said Elena. 'We shouldn't need too much rock.'

'But won't it just fall through?' asked Tima.

'I've got some metal too—old grilles and scrap from the

209

back of the car wash,' said Matt. 'We'll bridge the hole with that and pile the rocks on top.'

'But this is a *GOD* we're talking about,' said Tima. 'How is a pile of rocks going to stop it?'

'It's not the DLG it needs to stop—it's the song of the beam,' said Matt. 'Or the light. Or the electromagnetic field or whatever it gives off. The book in the library said old underworld gods can be disturbed by stuff up on the surface, if you believe that kind of thing. Which we do. So when the beam comes through it's attracting the DLG up to the surface.'

'Like rain bringing up worms,' said Elena. 'Massive, scary, death-inflicting worms.' She shivered.

'It might not work,' said Matt. 'But have you got a better idea?'

Tima was silent for a while. Then she said: 'All this rock? Have we got to drag it along the back, going over all those fences? That'll take *forever*.'

'I know,' said Matt. 'That's why I brought these babies.' He reached back behind the driver's seat and pulled out a pair of heavy-duty bolt cutters. 'For the gates.'

'God, you are *such* a crim!' laughed Elena.

'We get the moths to cover the cameras and lights again,' said Matt. 'And I break us in so we can drive right through. Then we only have to cart all the rocks down the side alley to the back of the warehouse.'

But it wasn't that simple. When they reached the approach to Quarry End they could see a light on in the security booth. Matt pulled off-road and drove them bumpily under their usual patch of holly trees. They all peered through the windscreen across to the gate. The guy with the clipboard was *there*. In the middle of the night. And he wasn't alone. Another security guy was with him, leaning in through the window from outside, chatting and smoking.

'They just keep getting more security guys,' murmured Elena. 'What if they see us?!'

'They won't,' said Tima. 'We'll distract them. Matt—I can send insects, but birds might be better. My guys might not be able to set off an alarm, but I bet your guys could.'

'Um . . . I don't know,' Matt said. 'They might.'

'Ask Lucky to help,' said Elena. 'You said she would be here, didn't you? Call her and ask her.'

Matt took a deep breath, wound down the window, and then called, softly: 'Lucky . . . are you here?' For a few worrying seconds silence settled all around them. And then there was a sudden flurry of wings, and a dark shape dropped from the branches above and on to Matt's shoulder. He grinned from ear to ear. 'You're *here*!'

The starling cocked her head sideways and fixed him with a beady stare.

'Can you help us?' said Matt. 'We need to distract those men over there . . . the ones in the booth. We need an alarm to go off right across the other side of Quarry End so they'll run off to check it out. Can your friends make that happen?'

The starling lifted her wings. 'Wait!' said Matt. He looked at his watch. 'I want your help—but I don't want your friends—your *family*—anywhere near here after one fifteen. I don't want any of you going into the Sentry warehouse when the beam comes through. I don't want any more birds to die. I want you all *safe*—do you understand me?'

'Safe,' said Lucky.

'So . . . please help us. Keep those guys chasing false alarms away from this end of the estate so we can get to the back of the warehouse, all right? About three alarms in a row should do it. Then take your flock far away to somewhere safe, before the beam comes. OK?'

'OK,' said Lucky.

They watched a dark cloud shimmer out of the trees above them and move, like one entity, across the estate. The men on the gate didn't notice this—but they did notice the alarm that went off a minute later and both hurried away to investigate.

'Right,' said Matt, as soon as they were out of sight. 'Let's go.'

A few metres deeper into the trees, Spin rubbed his sore hands and tried to make sense of what he'd seen and heard. He was capable of some pretty impressive special effects himself (his favourite was the sinister black smoke), but he had to admit the whole 'possess a flock of starlings' thing was a neat trick.

The need to know more was burning inside him. Painfully. The old books had turned up some interesting stuff, but he was still in the dark about so much. Being in the dark was his thing—but this kind was driving him nuts.

He watched them break in. First a sudden gloom descended as millions of insects swarmed the nearby street lights. Then

Car-wash Boy got a pair of bolt cutters, snapped through the security chains, and pushed the double gates open. What for? What did they want in there?

He didn't want to tangle with them just yet; he was still tired. But now he'd heard about some bird-killing beam going into the Sentry warehouse after one fifteen, well, he owed it to himself to check *that* out.

He waited and watched as they pulled in past the gates, then Mona Lisa jumped out and pushed the gates back together, looping the chain around them to look as if it hadn't been broken. Clever. Then she got back in, and the little truck drove on into the estate, taking its weird cloak of dimness with it. Well, he had his own cloak of dimness, so, after a couple of minutes, he headed directly for Sentry SuperSacks where something much more exciting than bubble wrap awaited him.

CHAPTER 38

Getting the rubble in was hard work. Matt had already done a lot of the work—pre-filling six thick blue vinyl sacks with it. There was an extra sack with bits of metal poking out. It took them a sweaty, punishing half hour to drag it all into the upper chamber.

As Elena and Matt lay exhausted on the floor for a minute, Tima stood up. She didn't need to stoop under the lower underhangs. She ran the torch beam around, gazing at the ripples of rock above them. 'It's amazing nobody's found this before,' she said.

'The entrance used to be overgrown,' said Elena. 'The DLG must have punched through all that.'

'Where's the weird blue light coming from?'

'It seems to be just in the rock,' said Elena. 'Maybe it's a kind of phosphorescence . . . you know, that living stuff that glows in the dark.'

'Come on,' said Matt, getting up. 'We haven't got long. We have to get down there and bung up that plughole before the beam comes.'

They slid carefully down into the lower chamber, and Tima grabbed Elena's hand as she gazed in awe at the dark-light well. 'I can see them,' she whispered.

The wisps were back—reaching around one end of the opening like curls of mist. They made Tima think of the fingers of a sea anemone, drifting innocently in the gentle water, just until a hapless shrimp came close enough to be grabbed and devoured.

Matt pulled a rusty grille from one of the sacks and laid it gently across the hole, pushing it across from the side furthest from those dark-light wisps. It was something off the front of an old car and big enough to reach from one side to the other. The wisps moved a little more agitatedly, twisting slightly as if caught in an air current. 'Keep it slow and steady,' said Elena. 'And stay calm. Don't juice those things up.'

It was pathetically easy to break into. The office door was just a matter of a blade and a bent pin. He was inside in under a minute. The security alarm gave three feeble bleeps before he disabled it with a pair of high-strength magnets. If any camera captured him, it wouldn't show much; just a cowled figure; faceless.

The warehouse was reached through an even flimsier door with no lock at all. The clock on the wall said 1.14 a.m.

This beam thing was due soon. Where, exactly? It was a large building.

He trod softly through the shadowy aisles, using the fine silver torch he kept in his coat pocket for just such occasions as these. He was a practised burglar, although he rarely stole anything. He didn't go into homes; that wouldn't work for him. But shops, offices, business premises—these were different. They were all an open invitation: fair game for his solitary wanderings.

The police cordon tape he'd seen last night had been taken away from the front of the building, but he wondered if there was something left inside to give him a clue about where the warehouse man had died. That had to be linked to Car-wash Boy's fear of birds dying. Maybe there was some kind of gas leak. But if so, surely there would have been public alerts; specialists in protective suits and masks. It would have been all over the news.

No. It was something else. Something even the coroner couldn't explain because Spin had been monitoring the news and seen nothing about the unexplained death yet. Usually post-mortem reports were back within a day. Not this time.

A sickly smell caught his attention. Ah. There it was. A small shrine. Half a dozen bunches of flowers lay on the floor by a fire escape door. There were handwritten messages on cards, as if the dead man could peer down from a heavenly cloud and thumb through them appreciatively.

The door. Was this where the fabled beam entered? He stepped over the flowers and opened it, pushing down hard on the alarm bar. The alarm did not sound; it was connected to the box he'd disabled in the office. Instead, some night air flowed in, and he peered out on to a dead end. The fire escape was barely fit for purpose; the cliff face and a broken chicken-wire fence were only a few steps on the other side of it. Not much space for escaping fire. Looking left and right through the gloom, he could make out wood-panelled fences at both corners. He took a step and felt it crunch.

'Now that is *distasteful*,' he murmured, lifting his boot. Beneath it was a pile of corpses. Birds, rats, mice, insects. Their eyes were eerily reflective, and he thought for one fleeting, idiotic moment that they were still alive and just pretending to be dead. A chill reached him. What the hell?! The eyes weren't just reflective . . . they were *red*.

Matt had something that looked like an oven shelf in his hands now. He leaned down and carefully rested it across the grille, creating a rough metal cross. Then he unrolled a bit of steel mesh and pressed it slowly on top of the rest. The wisps juddered and twisted, wriggling through the gaps in the collage of metal. He stepped back and took a long breath.

'Don't let them touch you,' whispered Elena.

Tima looked at her watch. 'It's no good,' she said. 'We haven't got time! The beam will be here in two minutes!'

'We can empty all these sacks and run in two minutes!' protested Matt.

'No,' said Elena. 'It's too risky. We're out of time. We'll have to come back again later—when the beam has passed through. If we're still here when it wakes up the—'

'No—we *can*—' Matt tried to lift and upend a rubble sack, but Elena grabbed his arm.

'We go NOW!' she hissed and ran to the dark seam of quartz, scaling the chamber wall in seconds. 'NOW!'

Matt finally saw sense. Cursing, he dumped the sack and ran.

They hurtled out through the upper chamber, crawling through the tunnel and out into the open air with 20 seconds to spare. 'Go! Go! Go!' bawled Matt, hot on Tima's heels as she pounded after Elena along the side alley. They reached the truck and got inside just as the singing rang through their heads.

It took a lot to give someone like *him* the creeps, but as he pulled the fire door shut again and stood alone in the warehouse, he got an overwhelming sense of top-grade, five-star, *undiluted* creepiness.

Spin closed his eyes, steadying himself.

Next, weirdly, he thought he heard singing.

Then the beam came, and he forgot everything.

For a few seconds they sat still, mesmerized behind the windscreen. Then they *felt* rather than saw the dark-light god. 'We should go!' Elena said, in a cracked, scared voice.

Matt broke out of his daze and gunned the engine, glad they'd reversed the truck in. He pulled away down the narrow side alley towards the main estate, but not before he saw, in the rear-view mirror, a dark-light tentacle writhe around the far corner of the warehouse. Where the security guards were now he no longer cared; he just had to get them all out of there.

CHAPTER 39

Spin was still clinging to a shelf when the beam died away. Several flying creatures lay stunned on the floor in front of him: two gulls and at least three pipistrelle bats. The beauty of the beam had brought hot tears to his eyes and made him sway and swoon along with the animals, but moments after the song echoed away, something else arrived in the warehouse and chilled his dark blood.

Something was coming through the door. Something shadowy and sick and full of grimness was leeching through the gaps around the bolts of the exit bar, dripping down the cracks on either side, creeping low beneath the threshold. Before he could find words for its shape, it gathered itself together in a tangle of tentacles. Like something from the deepest ocean, where light never shines, it pulsed and quivered, and then its tentacles flung forward and skewered through the birds and bats, swiping the life force from them in a split second.

It didn't stop there. It was now probing the air, blindly, seeking more prey. Spin felt his belly drop and his ears clog up with pressure. Acid shot through his veins, signalling the stark message 'RUN!'

Spin turned and fled. And the tentacled darkness behind him let out a noise that was half howl, half laughter. The warehouse aisle seemed very, very long. He ran, his earlier weakness bashed aside by the panic pouring through him. The panic and the disbelief. This did not happen. This did not happen to *him*.

He reached the office and found the door had swung shut. He grabbed at it, but his hands, slick with sweat, could not turn the orb-shaped handle. Terror was roaring in his ears . . . or maybe it was the tentacled thing roaring. Roaring and screaming with insane laughter. Roaring and screaming and smacking its horrific lips. Was this what the warehouseman had heard before—STOP IT STOP IT OPEN THE DOOR OPEN THE DOOR!!!

He swiped his palms across his coat and tried again, glancing back to see the tentacles riding the shelves, shooting up and down and then slapping and slithering along the floor at ever greater speed. Somewhere in the gloom behind them were flat red eyes and a gaping, grinning, black-toothed mouth.

DOOR!! He got a grip and flung it open, bounded through the lobby, slipped the latch he'd left up on the outer exit, and threw himself out into the night. The pale orange glow of the Quarry

End street lights gave him comfort for three or four seconds until he looked back and saw the dark tentacles were following him, right through the door, along the concrete, hissing and chuckling and murmuring with delight. Spin ran for the security booth, lit up in the distance. There were people there. Normal people. People from the normal world. This abnormal thing could not keep up its chase, surely, in front of normal people from the normal world.

He sprinted, drawn by the light and the shape of a man behind the glass. The gates were bent and flung open, and a broken metal chain lay like a dead snake on the ground. The other man was off to his right, running along the perimeter with his torch, heading for the gate, and talking into a two-way radio. In the corner of his eye, Spin saw a tentacle. It was parallel with him. It was overtaking him. It was distracted by the torchlight.

'HEY YOU! RUN FASTER! RUN! RUN!' he bawled through the night air. He saw the torchlight dance crazily. Heard a scream and then . . . a scream silenced.

He tore across to the security booth, pounded the window with his fists, risked three seconds' delay to yell: 'Don't go over there! JUST RUN! RUN!' He fled on through the bent gates. Over his shoulder he saw the man in the booth emerge and yell for his colleague. He saw the grim light of the tentacled creature slip backwards, retreating to the warehouse. The second man might survive. The first was dead, of that he was sure. And it was just split-second chance that it hadn't been him.

CHAPTER 40

Matt brought the truck to a lurching halt in a dark lay-by
a couple of streets from Tima's house and switched off the
headlights. 'Everyone OK?'

He turned to look at his passengers. They were both
gripping their upper seat belts. In the dim light, their faces were
masks of shock.

'I can't believe you just did that,' squeaked Tima.

Elena shook her head, looking waxy white. Neither of them
had let go yet.

'The gate was half-open anyway,' said Matt, trying to
sound nonchalant, despite his every limb shaking with
adrenaline. 'And if I hadn't sped up that guard guy would have
stopped us, and we'd all be waiting for the police to show up.
Game over.'

'You . . . you did the right thing,' gulped Elena. 'But . . . what if he hadn't got out of the way?'

'He was *always* going to get out of the way,' said Matt. 'Haven't you ever played chicken before? One person always moves. And, by the way, that person is never me.'

'What if he took down our number plate?' breathed Tima, slowly letting go of the seat belt and slumping into the seat.

'Don't worry. The plates are temporary,' said Matt.

Elena and Tima stared at him incredulously.

'They're magnetic. Look—Dad got them off this geezer in the motor trade. I knew where he kept them, so I attached them, front and back, over the real ones, before I even got in the truck tonight.' And he got out and pulled the plates off the front and back of the truck and flung them into the depths of the undergrowth.

'Total crim,' sighed Tima.

'Good job,' said Elena.

'I'm more worried about the scratch on the bumper,' said Matt, getting back in behind the wheel. 'But this is such a beaten-up old piece of junk, I'm hoping it won't get noticed.'

'I've got to get to bed,' said Tima. 'Sun'll be up soon. What are we going to do next?'

'We have to go back,' said Elena, looking grimly determined. 'Earlier, this time—and get that rubble down. Can we meet up at midnight?'

'I don't know,' said Tima. 'My parents are usually up until gone eleven—and they'll be coming to see me at the concert in the town hall. I'll be late to bed as well.'

'Oh god—yes—the concert. I'm in it too,' said Elena. 'I'm playing my cornet in a quartet. Let's talk some more at the concert, then. We can meet up backstage. And Matt . . . is there any chance you can come to the concert too?'

'Me? Yeah, right.' He rolled his eyes. 'I'll see what I can do.'

They drove on and dropped Tima off. As they pulled out of her road police sirens wailed in the distance. Elena glanced around at Matt fearfully.

'Don't worry,' he said. 'They're not going to come to RichToffsVille to look for a speeding truck. They'll go straight downtown . . .'

'Where *we* live,' said Elena.

But the sirens seemed to be heading away, towards Quarry End, most likely.

Matt dropped Elena off and headed home through the silent streets. He parked the truck on the forecourt, where it had been before. Soon he would be up again, cleaning it. When Dad wasn't looking he would sneak a little white touch-up pen across the scratch the half-open gate had made.

Tumbling into bed a few minutes later, to the distant lullaby of his father's snores, he noticed Lucky was back, roosting on his windowsill. Seeing her there eased the stress in his head and limbs enough for sleep to claim him at last.

CHAPTER 41

Show night. Tima was fizzing with nervous energy. They'd rehearsed all afternoon at school, and now they were here at the town hall, excitedly clustered backstage with the other performers, and the show had already begun. The *Oliver!* songs were in the second half, so Mrs Theroux was only now helping them with costume and make-up. Tima was back in the familiar tight corseted dress with her hair piled up on her head, Victorian style. Her lips were painted pink, and her eyelashes were thick with mascara.

Across the dressing room, Elena was polishing up her cornet with a cloth. She smiled over, and Tima smiled back and crossed the old grey carpet to speak to her.

'When are you on?' she asked.

'We're second on after the interval,' said Elena. 'How are you doing? Nervous?'

'Oh yeah,' said Tima. 'Really nervous.'

'You don't look it. You look totally cool,' said Elena. 'You're brave, singing a solo. I'm really nervous playing mine, and it's only short.'

'I'm not nervous about *this*,' said Tima, waving her hand dismissively. 'Well—maybe a bit—but I'm much *more* nervous about . . . you know. Tonight.' She leaned in closer and murmured. 'We've got to finish the job.'

'We will,' said Elena. 'We have to.'

Tima nodded. 'I just wish we'd done it last night.' She shivered. 'He was killed instantly; that's what the news report said. Another dead man in Quarry End. It might have been that security guy we met—the one in the booth.'

Elena nodded, keeping her voice as low as Tima's. 'It's been all over the news. People are starting to notice now—starting to investigate. Even kids at school were talking about it today. There's a rumour going round that he was struck by lightning. In the middle of a summer's night with no rain! I wish it were true.'

'So do I,' said Tima, solemnly. 'But we know what it really was. I bet he had those red eyes when they found him, poor guy.'

'I hope that truck has been collected from the car wash now,' said Elena. 'It got mentioned on the news. If they track it down and link it to Matt . . . they might think *he's* something to do with what happened to that guard.'

'Different plates,' said Tima, shrugging. 'The registration number won't match.' She became aware that Lily and her mates were staring at her, wondering why she was chatting to a

Harcourt High School student. 'Is Matt here?'

'Yes,' said Elena. 'He's in the audience. He told his mum and dad one of his mates was performing, and they said he could come and watch. I don't think he told them *which* mate. I'll slip outside in the interval and see how he's doing. What do you think about meeting at midnight?'

Tima shook her head. 'I'm worried about Mum and Dad not being asleep—but I think we have to go for it. We can't wait until later.'

She went back to Mrs Theroux, who wanted to put extra hairspray on her.

'Who was that you were talking to?' asked Lily, as soon as Mrs Theroux had gone to stick Fagin's moustache on.

'Oh, just a friend,' said Tima. 'She's playing in the brass and woodwind group.'

'She goes to Harcourt, doesn't she?' said Lily, pulling a face.

'Yes,' said Tima. 'And . . . ?'

Lily shrugged and laughed. 'My mother says the girls at Harcourt High are all jealous of us because we get a better education.'

'Well, *my* mother says the girls at Harcourt High are all sorry for us, because we have to wear stupid hats,' countered Tima.

'Anyone would think you don't *like* Prince William Prep,' said Lily. 'Maybe you'd fit in better at the chavvy school.'

Tima was about to say something stinging back, but Lily suddenly started shrieking and flapping. 'Ugh! Ugh! Get it off me!' A wasp had flown in through the open window and was seriously buzzing her.

Keira and Clara immediately started panicking—screaming and flapping at the poor creature with their show programmes. It was getting angry and even more likely to sting one of them. Tima took a deep breath and called to it. It turned in mid-air and flew to her outstretched hand. It landed on her palm and sat there, feelers waving agitatedly.

'Ugh! Quick! Someone—it's on Tima! Kill it!' shrieked Lily.

Tima felt the strongest urge to ask the wasp to sting Lily's stupid, mean face. The wasp began to take off from her palm, quite willing. She hastily told it *no*. She did not want to cause more mayhem. More than that, she did not want her little stripy friend to get squashed. She blew gently on the wasp and guided it back out through the window.

Clara chased after it with her rolled-up programme and then said: 'It's OK—it's gone. Eurgh! I *hate* wasps! They're so disgusting. Honestly—what's the *point* of them?'

'What's the point of *you*?' asked Tima.

Really, she wasn't doing herself any favours here.

Elena found Matt near the stage, looking ill at ease as kids, teachers, and families wandered around getting interval drinks and chatting. She guessed going out to watch a charity concert wasn't really on his to-do list on any normal day. But she also guessed there wasn't going to *be* a normal day again for any of them. She was both sad and glad Mum hadn't felt able to come tonight. It would have been hard to explain why she was seeking out a Year 9 boy.

'This isn't your usual night out, is it?' she said, smiling as she sat down in the chair just behind him, her backpack, with the cornet inside, slung over one shoulder.

'What? Oh—this? No, not really.' He turned around to look at her.

Elena narrowed her eyes at him. 'What's up? I was thinking you were spooked by all the arty-farty types, but it's not that, is it?'

'No,' he said. He looked squarely at her. 'I keep thinking I see dark-light. We've *got* to get back and seal that hole.'

Elena felt chilled. 'The DLG doesn't come out this early,' she said.

He shook his head. 'I'm probably imagining it. I've been obsessing about it all day.' He looked at her as if he badly wanted her to agree with that. 'I keep thinking about that security guy in Quarry End last night. *Another* death. It's doing my head in. Maybe if we hadn't been messing about in the cave we wouldn't have drawn it out.'

She nodded. 'I know. I thought that too. But we weren't there before the first guy got killed, were we? Who knows what it does once the beam wakes it up? It would probably have come outside anyway.'

'I think that stupid vampire wannabe was there too,' muttered Matt. 'Some of the news reports said there was another witness the police were trying to find—a boy with blond hair, in dark clothes, shouted at the other guard; told him to run. Sound familiar . . . ?'

'It does.'

'They'll be hunting him down as a suspect, too,' said Matt.

'I don't think *he'd* kill anyone,' she said.

'No? You thought he was a *real* vampire the other night!'

She stared around the town hall, not wanting to argue about Spin. Matt thought he was their enemy, and he was probably right, but she wasn't sure *what* Spin was. She certainly didn't trust him—but she had to admit he did fascinate her. A little.

The old square auditorium was packed out for the charity concert. 'I can't see any dark-light,' she said. 'We're all so tired; it could just be your brain playing tricks.' But she was now sharing his fear. It occurred to her that this building was very close to Quarry End. In fact ... 'Wait a minute.' She dug into her school blazer pocket and pulled out the folded map she'd drawn her line on a few nights back. 'Come and look at this,' she said, leading Matt across to the front of the stage which jutted out beyond the closed curtains. People milled about with plastic cups of tea and snacks but paid them no attention. She spread the map out on the edge of the stage and ran her finger along the line.

'Matt—look,' she said, and he peered across her shoulder. The line she'd drawn, running from the car wash to her house, on through Tima's, and straight into Sentry SuperSacks ... it also intersected one corner of Thornleigh Town Hall.

CHAPTER 42

Dark-light or no dark-light, Tima was sure of one thing. No underworld god was going to get in the way of her solo *this* time.

Elena had fed back Matt's fears just before she'd gone onstage to play with her quartet. In the wings Tima had watched her friend perform a five-minute medley, note-perfect, despite her eyes constantly roaming the hall throughout. Elena was so distracted it was amazing she didn't mess up her solo. As she came back offstage, Tima had grabbed her hand and whispered. 'Well done! See anything . . . ?'

Elena had scooped up her bag and whispered back: 'I don't know. It's hard to tell with the stage lights on.'

Tima was depending on that now as they danced and sang through their show numbers. She refused to look. If the DLG was coming for them it could blinking well wait until she'd sung her song. The first two numbers went really well and received warm applause and a bit of whooping and whistling. She got all her dance steps right and even managed to smile at Lily, who was shooting mean looks at her every chance she got.

At last the spotlight fell on Tima, and the opening notes of 'As Long as He Needs Me' struck out across a hushed audience.

She took a deep breath and sang her first line. And her voice rang out clear and true and filled with emotion. Her nerves were in check; adrenaline was doing its job—powering her up to her utmost performance. No moth was ever going to bother her again. *Nothing* was going to wreck the next three minutes.

The audience was spellbound. In the front few rows she could see their faces—rapt and held. One or two were mopping their eyes. Mum and Dad were grinning with pride and encouragement. Mr James was glancing up from his piano keyboard, beaming with delight. *This.* This moment. This was all her own.

Then she saw it. High up in the corner of the tall windows that arched along the town hall auditorium on either side. There it was. Across the sky outside. A flicker . . . like lightning.

Dark-lightning.

Dread filled her chest. The corset seemed very tight. Still she sang. The song rang on out of her, and there was no noticeable change in her delivery, but the adrenaline was spiking up—and it had good reason to. It didn't care about her song. It was telling her to run. She was seriously considering it, eyeing the doors and windows.

And that's when the sky outside exploded.

CHAPTER 43

The boom shook the glass in all the town hall windows, and one or two of them shattered, but it was the flash of white light that made the audience gasp and a few of them scream. Tima abandoned her solo and ran to the edge of the stage to see better out of the high arched side windows. The audience was shaken and murmuring, and many people were getting to their feet. The lady mayor ran on to the stage, grabbed a microphone from the stand, and said: 'Everybody! Please stay calm! It looks like there's been an incident at the power station, but we should be quite safe in this building.'

Tima saw Elena and Matt at the nearest side window, picked up her Victorian skirts, and ran down the steps, stage left, to get to them. Despite the reassurances of the mayor and the shouts of teachers and parents that the children should stay where they were, there was a rush of people now trying to see outside. The sky was lit with a pulsing cloud of pink. The chimney stack on the power station was engulfed in flame.

Tima grabbed her friends' arms, pressing her nose against the window, staring hard through the glass. As they were jostled by more appalled sightseers, shouting for news and wailing about terrorist attacks, all three of them were mute; eyes fixed on the tower. The flame at the top did not bother them.

The dark-light tentacle curling up the chimney beneath did.

'Oh god,' murmured Elena, faintly.

'Not *this* god,' grunted Matt. 'I *knew* we should have finished sealing that hole last night. I *knew* it.'

'What does it want?' breathed Tima.

Suddenly more light shafted into the auditorium. Many people were filing away into the foyer at the back, but some had opened the fire escape doors and were moving outside to stare up at the flaming power station in awe. The spectacle, across a wide area of grassy wasteland, was just far enough away for people to feel safe to stand and stare. Emergency sirens were already rising above the hubbub of the crowd.

'You know what it wants,' said Matt. 'And it's out to get it.'

'What do you mean?' Elena's voice was trembling. She already knew. They all did.

Matt suddenly started elbowing his way through the crowd, pushing to the front to get out of the doors. 'It travels just so far,' he yelled back at Elena and Tima as they rudely shoved their way outside and scrambled to stay with him. 'It uses energy— gets fired up by all those things it kills! The birds pulled it into the warehouse. The warehouse guy powered it to the outside. It juiced itself up last night on that patrol guard, and now it's got out as far as the power station. And look—it's just waiting for everyone else to come to *it* now. It's deliberately calling attention to itself. It made a fire for attention. It *likes* the attention.' He gulped. 'There's going to be a massacre!'

'But nobody's going to run *towards* a fire,' said Tima. 'Surely?'

'No?' said Matt. 'Just look at them.'

Tima stared around at the people now milling about on the grass and low brick walls that surrounded the town hall. They were clustered in groups, many clinging to each other and talking fearfully; excitedly. Plenty of them had their smartphones out, filming—and some were starting to move closer, edging towards the wasteland that stretched between the perimeter of the power station and the car park behind the town hall, trying to get more dramatic images.

Across the growing cacophony of sirens, crowd noise, and distant flames, the mayor was shouting: 'EVERYBODY! It's not safe out here! There may be fumes! You all need to come back inside.'

But nobody was paying any attention. Parents had reclaimed their children from the stage and dressing rooms, and family huddles had formed, but nobody seemed to want to move back inside; they were all too mesmerized by the flaming chimney. Several people had now got a lot bolder and *were* running towards the fire, excited by the flashing blue lights now marking a line down the access road on the other side of the power station site.

'Can't they *see* that thing?' said Elena, pointing at the dark-light tentacles writhing at the base of the chimney.

'The mayor's right,' said Matt. 'We've got to get them away from that thing. Back into the town hall. He turned to stare at Tima. 'DO something!'

Tima gaped at him for a few seconds, wondering what he meant. And then she cottoned on and took a deep breath. She could hear Mum and Dad calling for her, further back in the crowd. If she was going to do something, it had to be now.

She closed her eyes and sent a message to a particular insect. *Please. PLEASE. You need to help us! PLEASE! Come . . . come now!*

There was a buzzing as she pressed her eyes tightly closed. It grew louder and louder, and she did not know whether it was real or just in her head. Until the screaming started.

Elena grabbed her arm and held fast, breathing hard. 'Wow!' was all she said. Tima dared to open her eyes and saw a flickering black and yellow cloud descending on them. There must have been millions. Thousands of millions. *Millions* of millions. And they had come to help *her*.

'WASPS!' screamed someone, and Tima turned to see Lily and her friends staring wild-eyed with fear up into the sky. They were about to discover the *point* of wasps. The swarm was coming from the direction of the flaming tower, swirling like a tornado. It looked like the end of days, set against the towering inferno. The screaming picked up into a crescendo of panic, and everyone started to run back into the town hall. Tima turned to see her parents being swept along with the crowd and helplessly disappearing back inside through the open doors.

The wasps pushed everyone on, spreading out from the tornado and forming smaller squadrons to chase the panicked crowd back inside. She and Matt and Elena were the only people not running. Matt grabbed her hand and Elena's and pulled them both aside to stand in the shelter of some high privet hedging. The wasp storm raged *everywhere*, Tima's tiny winged shepherds pelting through the air like black and yellow raindrops.

Soon the three of them were outside alone, untouched by the swarm but horribly exposed to the underworld god. More tentacles were twisting out from the base of the chimney now, and they were definitely intent on reaching three terrified Night Speakers. Elena found herself pressing back into the hedge, her backpack containing her cornet in its case pushing into the leaves. She wished she could get right *inside* the hedge.

The sirens were getting louder. The line of blue flashing lights revealed the emergency services were entering the power station grounds by the main gate on the far side of its enclosure.

'If they reach the tower,' said Matt. 'They're dead.'

'What can we do?' said Elena, her voice high with fear against the buzzing and the distant shrieks from the town hall. 'What can we *do*?'

'For a start, darling, you might want to take *that* out of your backpack.'

They all spun around, startled, to see a dark figure with pale, luminous skin push out of a gap in the privet hedge. Matt gave a growl as soon as he recognized him. 'I thought we told you—'

'Shut up, SpongeBob,' said Spin. 'Elena—get your trumpet out.'

Elena gaped and then said: 'It's a *cornet*, not a trumpet. And anyway . . . are you *insane?*'

'Probably,' he said, swiping a wasp away from his face. 'But it might be the only thing that's going to get that ugly string of slime back where it belongs. That or maybe Little Miss Songbird here.'

'What are you *talking* about?' said Tima, staring up at him.

'Could you just tell your little helpers to stop dive-bombing me?' he asked, swatting another.

Tima glanced around the others, shocked. He *knew?*

'Yes—I've worked it out, sweetheart. I've been stalking you all long enough. Er . . . please . . . ?'

'He's OK,' said Tima. 'Leave him.' And the wasps flew off to other duties.

Spin gave her a mocking bow. 'Thank you, Princess. Now—we'd better get to that thing before our local heroes do.'

'Whoa!' said Matt, shoving Spin against the hedge. 'Who made *you* boss? And what makes you think we trust a word you say?'

Elena stared from Matt to Spin. 'Just wait, Matt—I want to hear it.'

'Really? How do you know he's not some kind of dark-light monkey working for *that?*' said Matt, flinging an arm back towards the flaming tower.

'I've *met* that,' Spin snapped. 'And I *don't* want to meet it again. This is *my* town, and I don't want it annihilated any more than you do!'

'So—you're helping us, are you?' sneered Matt, bouncing

on the balls of his feet and simmering with rage. 'In return for *what*? *Blood*?!' He gave a derisory snicker.

'Listen, Turtle Wax,' hissed Spin. 'Now is not the time. I find imminent Armageddon takes the edge off my thirst.'

'What the hell?' gasped Elena. 'Look—stop it, both of you. LOOK!'

They all followed her trembling finger. The DLG was still clinging to the base of the tower, its tendrils curling and stabbing through the air in the direction of the approaching fire crews. And on the wasteland between the power station perimeter and where they stood, *everything* was moving.

The wildlife was fleeing.

Mice, rats, voles, rabbits, foxes, even some burly badgers, were all streaking across the wasteland. Bats and birds flitted low across the long grass. An exodus, but not from the fire. A chimney fire would never have freaked out the animal world like this. She felt as much as she saw Velma rush past—and pause—and gaze from her cubs to her human friend. *Thank you—but GO!* Elena sent, and she felt a wave of relief from the vixen as she ran on with her young.

'Oh dear,' said Spin. 'That's not good. Perhaps you'd like to listen to me now?'

'What? What can we do?' demanded Elena.

'It's a god—you know that, yes?'

'Yes, of course we know that,' snapped Tima. 'That's probably how *you* know.'

'Well, I probably know more about underworld gods than you do,' he snapped back. 'They love a bit of catastrophe. They

239

thrive on it. The more screaming and panic and horror they can cause, the better the party.'

'We *have* worked that out,' muttered Matt, eyeing Spin with such loathing, Tima thought he might punch him at any moment.

'So, the only thing a god likes better—maybe—than catastrophe is a little worship,' said Spin. 'So Tima, how about a song . . . ?'

'Er . . . what?' said Tima.

'You know—something an underworld god might like,' said Spin. 'Anything will do—just try to look as if you mean it. It must be pretty bored with all the screaming by now. Surprise it.'

Matt let out a volley of expletives, but Tima stepped away from the hedge and began to walk towards the power station.

'Tima!' yelled Matt. 'What are you doing? Come back!'

'Have you got a better idea?' she called back. Then she took another deep breath and began her second solo that evening.

CHAPTER 44

The tentacles writhing around the chimney looked much more solid than they had before, as she drew closer to the high perimeter fence. Spiky dark-light wisps spun out from them, snatching at falling embers as they drifted down from the flaming stack above.

Tima tried to imagine she was back onstage. Tried to remember the joy and serenity she had felt just ten minutes ago, before hell on earth kicked off. What to sing? What would butter up a god of dark-light? She thought for a moment and then took a deep breath. Doing all she could to keep the shake out of her voice, she let rip with the cheesiest anthem that sprang to mind. Westlife's hit 'You Raise Me Up' rang out in her steady, high voice, sweet and clear against the cacophony.

It was laughable. Lyrics of love and admiration. Could an underworld god detect the lie? Any moment now it was going to let out an insane cackle and kill her with a swipe of one tentacle.

'No—*let her!*'

She was aware of a fight going on behind her as Spin and Matt struggled to control the situation.

'Elena! No!'

And then Elena was next to her, raising the gleaming curves of her cornet and adding some clear, sweet, low notes to her song. Spin and Matt were on either side of them now, staring up at the dark-light god as they all moved, insanely, step after step closer.

And maybe it *wasn't* insane because Tima suddenly realized, as she reached the key change, that the tentacles were writhing less, and some red eyes in the nebulous dark-light of its face were slightly less crazed. Maybe Spin was *right*.

It was looking at her. Looking at *Elena too.* And it was quiet.

For a few golden seconds, she thought they might survive this.

There was a sudden burst of noise and activity beyond the perimeter fence.

'Oh no,' moaned Matt, as three fire tenders emerged on the concrete access area to the tower and their crew tumbled out, fluorescent uniforms and helmet visors gleaming in the firelight, shouting to each other and running to set up the water jets. 'STOP!' he yelled. 'GO BACK!'

Abruptly the DLG snapped its attention round to the newcomers. None of them, it seemed, could hear Matt's warning shouts. And none could see the tentacles reaching down towards them, ready to play.

'Just keep going!' came a terse voice. Spin.

But Tima's voice was stuck in her throat as she saw the closest firefighter fall. Her hands flew to her mouth. She couldn't stop this. She had been stupid to think she could.

CHAPTER 45

Matt sprinted to the perimeter fence and screamed at the firefighters to run, but if they heard him they didn't react. Two of them were stooping over the fallen guy, oblivious to the snaking tentacle waving just above their heads.

'HEY! HEY *YOU*!' bawled Matt. But he wasn't yelling at the fire and rescue crew now. He was yelling at the god of dark-light. 'OVER HERE, YOU OVERGROWN MAGGOT!'

The massive entity paused and turned its red eyes on Matt. He capered about on the concrete as the fire belched pink clouds overhead, and the dark-light god slid a dozen more tentacles down the base of the chimney shaft and across the ground towards him. A feral roar of delight was emerging from it.

He heard Tima cry, 'What is he *doing*?'

Matt glanced over his shoulder and yelled, 'I should have

poured on the rubble!' His voice cracked. 'I should have! It's my fault.'

He rushed towards a tentacle as it curled and quivered just a car's length away, and then ran back again, like a child on a beach, dodging the incoming waves.

'You're going to get *eat-en*,' Spin sang out. 'Go ahead! It's all good for me—*I* can look after the ladies now, Car-wash Boy!'

Matt ran right at him then, head lowered, fists up, boiling with rage. And Spin shot out his left leg and expertly flipped him. Matt sprawled on to a weed-strewn lump of concrete but sprang up again ready for the fight. Spin seized him in a steely grip and pulled him in close. 'We can do this another time,' he hissed. 'IF there *is* another time.'

Before Matt could struggle away Elena and Tima yelped with fear. The tentacles were nearly upon them, and, worse, the full face of the dark-light god finally showed itself, peeping around the base of the tower with a horrific grin. If some ancient sea monster had looked at itself in a shattered mirror, it might have seen what they saw. A smashed-up face with several burningly insane eyes and a torn mouth full of blackened needle-sharp teeth, encircling a rolling, engorged, putrid green tongue, dripping with mucus.

They all screamed then. Even Spin. Then he turned to Matt and yelled in his ear: 'Get your birds back here! Get them now!'

Matt tried to protest. Why would he want a thousand dead starlings on his conscience?

'We NEED them!' Spin was gripping his shoulders and shaking him, and, although Matt *hated* the boy, something in

245

him knew he was right. So before he could stop himself he asked.

Seconds later the downdraught of thousands of wingbeats struck them.

'YOU TOO!' cried Spin to Elena, who was staring, mouth open and cornet hanging limply in one hand. 'Get your foxes and your dogs and anything else that's willing.'

CHAPTER 46

Elena felt the call leave her mind. *Help me. Help us. PLEASE.* Within seconds she felt the push of warm bodies against her legs. Velma was there, and she hadn't come alone. There were at least thirty foxes and as many badgers, a small herd of deer, and more rabbits, weasels, stoats, rats, and mice than she could ever count. Dogs too and even cats, their fur on end and tails twitching. The wasteland was filled with mammals—all terrified—all ready to help.

'Make them do something,' said Spin. 'They need to impress that thing. Soon.'

The tentacles were whirling through the air towards them like a nightmare spin dryer.

Elena drew a breath. 'BOW!' she screamed.

Overhead the starlings swooped and swirled in a dazzling

display, a glittering cloud, lit by fire. Matt stood with his arms aloft like the conductor of an orchestra. His birds formed curls and loops, mirroring the tentacles, but somehow making them beautiful. Slower. More graceful.

Elena gaped. Then she dropped her eyes to the ground and gave a cry of amazement. It was filled with thousands of her friends. And they all, from the tallest stag to the tiniest mouse, were quite still. Facing the horror. Heads bowed.

A silence fell. Beyond it the emergency crews were still working, aiming pressured jets of water on to the blazing chimney. But here on the wasteland everything seemed to be suspended in time. Even the stag beetles gently circling over Tima's head were silent.

The god of dark-light paused. Its horrifying face seemed to settle in repose. The tentacles slowed and drifted like weeds in a slow-moving river.

'Is this what you want?' cried Elena. 'Is this *enough* for you?'

She felt her insides shrivel as its gaze fell upon her. It let out a long, long exhalation. A single, thin tentacle wriggled through the air towards her. Everyone froze. Even Spin seemed to have run out of words. Elena raised her hands, the cornet still clutched in one, and held back a whimper. The tentacle wound around the curves of the instrument, travelling the gleaming brass. Elena stared at it, terror holding her motionless, and felt dark-light energy thrumming through the metal.

The word that came to her seemed to travel up from her feet and shake her internal organs with its deep, deep bass rumble.

'MORE.'

She put the mouthpiece to her lips, where it juddered against her chattering teeth. A few high shrieks of pure fear escaped the instrument. *What if one of those gossamer-thin tentacles went inside the bell and wound up through the many twists and turns of brass, ducked under the valves . . . and poured straight down her throat?*

Then she felt fur against her legs and the wrap of a warm fox tail around her ankles. Velma was still there—in the most terrible danger, she had not run. Elena clamped down on her terror and played. 'Solveig's Song' from *Peer Gynt*. Melancholy and beautiful. Enough to soothe a god . . . ?

Its face grew closer. She could smell its rotten meat breath. She could see its horrific face crease into something that might be a smile.

Then she was seized.

Light flared through the sky. She felt herself grabbed and hurled around with such force it knocked the breath from her. She heard the others scream her name, saw them fly away below, birds and animals scattering in panic, as she was borne into the air. Then she was being dragged into the tentacles that were now retreating at speed, back and back, into the underworld they'd strayed from. Helpless, she was pulled through the burning night, past the fire and rescue crews, past the power station grounds, through the trees, through the fences and trucks and warehouses and rocks and back down, down, down into hell.

CHAPTER 47

'Wake up. Wake up, Mona Lisa. You're not done yet.'

Elena felt someone gently slapping at her face. She groaned and tried to roll over in bed and go back to sleep, but something cold and gritty was under her cheek. Suddenly, she sat up, fear assailing her as she realized she was not at home, under her quilt, but on the floor of a cave. *The* cave.

A pale blue glow lit the face of the person who was kneeling next to her.

'Spin . . . ?' she groaned. 'What are *you* doing here?' She sat up, aching and stinging all over.

'I followed you. Kind of,' he said. He was on his knees beside her. His silken black coat was ripped down one side, and there were dark smudges of blood across his hands. Looking up she saw more blood on his temple and grazes and bruises across his chin.

'What happened to *you*?' she mumbled, wincing as she tried to stand.

'I'd wait a while,' he said, pressing her back down again with one hand. His longest black fingernail was snapped right off. 'You're a bit bashed up yourself,' he added.

She became aware of stickiness on her face, around her mouth, and across her left ear. 'Oh,' she said, feeling a little dizzy. 'I'm bleeding. What happened? OH GOD!' Abruptly her memories flooded in, like greyhounds out of a trap. The dark-light god! The tentacles! The animals bowing . . . for *her*.

'Where are Matt and Tima?' she said, staring at Spin. 'And the animals? What happened to the animals?'

'Relax—the animals are gone. And Matt and Tima are in the hospital by now.'

'The hospital?!' she shrieked, leaping to her feet despite the dizziness.

'I said *relax*,' said Spin. 'They'll live. Probably. We all got flung into the air when our underworld friend took you. Tima and Matt were knocked out when they landed, but I wasn't. So I followed. Can't believe I didn't find this place last night. But it was easy to track you inside.'

'Why easy?' she asked.

'I could smell your blood. A positive, yes?'

Elena gulped. She was alone in a cave with a vampire. 'Look . . . I didn't invite you in,' she muttered.

'You didn't need to,' he said. 'It's not *your* cave. Anyway, your pretty neck is safe for now. I'm not in the mood. Later maybe. How come you're not lying here dead with red eyes?'

Elena struggled to remember. So much was a blur. She found her cornet at her feet. 'It stopped,' she said. 'It dropped me right here. I think . . . I think I played some more for it.'

Spin gaped at her and then shook his head, blinking. 'You mean to say it just wanted a private recital? My—you must be good.'

'I'm not *that* good,' she said. 'But . . .' she closed her eyes. It was like trying to piece together a dream. ' . . . it *liked* it. It liked the animals bowing and the birds dancing for it. You were right. We . . . *pleased* it.' She shuddered. 'It went back to sleep. *Pleased*.'

There was a moment of silence, and then Spin sniffed and said, 'Fine. Good work, you. Brilliant thinking, *me*.' He walked over to the hole and peered into the darkness beneath the heap of metal struts and grilles. 'Lucky he didn't take you down with him.'

Elena shivered.

'But just in case it comes back for more, I really think we need to get on to this now.' He pointed to the sacks of rubble beside the metal-strewn hole.

Elena blinked and then remembered. 'The beam,' she said. She snatched her wrist up and peered at her watch. It read: 00.03. 'It'll be here in an hour and a half.'

She got to her feet and grabbed a rubble sack. 'Let's go.'

It took a few minutes to upend all the bags and create a mound of rock, rubble, and metal across the hole. Once it was done they stood and looked at it.

'Can't help thinking that's pretty easy for an immortal entity to punch a hole through,' said Spin.

'I know,' said Elena. 'It's not for that. It's to stop it hearing—

or sensing—the beam when it comes through. We think that's what woke it up.'

Spin stood looking at the rubble and metal, unconvinced. 'Wait,' he said. 'I'll be back.'

Then he was gone, and she had nothing to do but sit and watch the untidy seal they had made across a hole into the underworld. She was very tired. Her vision swam in the thin blue light, and she tried not to think about Matt and Tima. Spin had said they were knocked out. He didn't seem worried about them, but then he probably didn't care about them. He didn't strike her as someone who *did* caring.

She was brought to full alertness by the sound of laboured breathing and a metallic scraping. Spin was back, clutching what looked like a couple of metal cylinders.

'What is *that*?'

He smirked. 'Oxy-acetylene welding torch. Obviously.'

'Where did you get it?' She shook her head, staggered.

'Castle Ironworks,' he said. 'Conveniently situated in Quarry End.' He knelt down, twisted some gauges on the canisters, and then, with a pop, produced a blue-white flame.

'You broke in and stole it?' she murmured.

'Erm . . . *you* just made a herd of mammals do your bidding,' he said, pulling some goggles across his eyes. 'And sent a killer god back to the underworld with a *tune*. Get some perspective.' And he blasted the rubble in flame.

It took about 20 minutes, taking turns, to finish the job. It was noisy, but no dark-light wisps came to check it out. Maybe she really *had* lullabied the god to sleep. The chalky rock and the metal slowly fused together and left a large pale scab, riven with red and black, where the hole had once been.

They stood back and looked at their work.

'Not exactly Italian marble,' said Spin. 'But it's not bad.'

'Now we just have to find out whether it works,' said Elena, checking her watch again. 'Nine minutes to go.'

They sat, resting against the cave wall, and waited.

'Do you really drink blood?' she asked after a minute of silence.

'Do you want to see my fangs?' he offered.

'Really, no,' she said.

When the beam came, it travelled over their heads and made her want to catch a hold and go with it. Could there exist anything more beautiful? When she came to, there were tears running down her face.

And nothing trying to break through the seal they'd made.

'I think we did it,' she whispered to Spin.

But Spin had gone.

CHAPTER 48

The big news story was the explosion: the power station that erupted into flame—and then the secondary explosion near its base that had scorched the neighbouring wasteland and concussed two kids and one firefighter. The wasps were great television too: there was plenty of shaky mobile phone footage of screaming people fleeing the swarm. And lots of astonished testimony that not one person had been stung. A famous wildlife expert was brought on to BBC Breakfast to explain this.

'Despite their bad reputation, wasps won't sting unless they absolutely have to,' he said, earnestly. 'And these wasps were merely trying to escape a threat—and that threat wasn't coming from the crowd below them. They probably had nests in the power station or in trees nearby and were just trying to get away.'

The presenter nodded. 'Of course, three days later we're still waiting to find out what caused the explosion,' she said. 'But the speculation is that it was a slow, undetected gas leak, which had built up over several days. There was also quite a stampede of wildlife, according to witnesses. Is that normal, would you say, Chris?'

'Animals have much better sense than humans when it comes to getting out of danger,' said Chris. 'They will migrate away from wildfires and floods and tsunamis—often well before humans are even aware of the threat. It is a bit surprising here in England, but not unheard of.'

Elena lay on the sofa under a blanket, woozily watching the TV and marvelling at the way nobody—*nobody*—was reporting the appearance of a terrifying underworld entity. There was no video of it—nothing from the helmet cams on the fire and rescue crew, even though the tentacles had come within a whisker of them and one guy had been left unconscious for a few minutes. They had been just as oblivious when she had walked back through Quarry End and past the fire they were subduing. All the emergency services had been focused on the chimney—including the police who had been on duty at the industrial estate, investigating that second security guard death and the runaway truck and the shadowy kid who'd shouted a warning. Nobody stopped her as she sloped past with her backpack and her cuts and bruises, hefting a bit of welding equipment, which she left tucked into the porch of Castle Ironworks (she couldn't help it; she was a good girl).

Her mother had slept through all the drama. She hadn't even been aware that Elena was still home the next morning until the school phoned up, doing a headcount on its students.

Elena slept, on and off, for two days. She told her mother about the fire and said it had been a shock, but also that she felt a bit fluey. Mum phoned Harcourt High back and said her daughter wouldn't be in until next week. She came in every so often with soup and buttered bread or tea and biscuits. Sinking back into sleep after each kindly interruption, Elena enjoyed the novelty of being looked after. She couldn't remember the last time her mum had been so . . . well . . . *mumsy*.

She had still woken at 1.34 a.m. the last two nights—felt the beam pass through—and then fallen asleep again. Occasionally she wondered about Matt and Tima but something inside told her they were OK and she was too exhausted to argue with it. Her dreams were dark and intense but getting less and less terrifying as she caught up on the lost sleep. The memories in them were being sorted and labelled and put into boxes marked: AMAZING, TERRIFYING, BAD, WONDERFUL, GOOD, WORRYING, TERRIBLE, and NOT NOW. Today she had awoken at 10 a.m. and felt recovered enough to come downstairs in her pyjamas, get under a blanket on the sofa, and watch TV with Mum.

'It's amazing more people weren't hurt,' Mum said, curled up at the other end of the sofa with a cup of tea. 'A boy from your school was taken to hospital, you know.'

'Was his name Matt?' asked Elena. She felt ashamed that she had not asked before. Or about Tima.

Mum opened her mouth to reply but was cut short by the doorbell going. Elena had a visitor.

'What happened to you?' Tima demanded, as soon as Elena's mum had left the room and gone out into the garden.

'I think we sent it away,' said Elena. 'And then we bolted the door.' She explained all that had occurred in the cave, including the welding session and the return of the beam . . . but not the DLG.

'You charmed a god,' said Tima. 'That's pretty cool.'

'You did too,' pointed out Elena. 'You were so brave, standing there, singing at it. So was Matt—trying to distract it from those fire crews. What happened to you and Matt?'

'Not completely sure,' said Tima. 'I remember being blown through the sky. Then I hit my head on something and didn't wake up until I was halfway to the hospital. Good job those emergency crews were right next to us! They had Matt in the ambulance with me; he didn't come round at all. I just got a mild concussion and scrapes and bruises. I think he got hurt a bit more. He'll be OK, though.'

'How do you know?' asked Elena, raising one eyebrow.

Tima glanced out of the window. 'Same way I knew *you* were OK. I heard it from the birds and the bees.'

Elena smiled. 'Hey—I've been sleeping. Lots. I think Mum might have slipped something into my food.'

'I've been sleeping too,' said Tima. 'Mum and Dad think it's a shock reaction.'

'Have they forgiven you for running off and getting yourself nearly killed?' asked Elena.

Tima grinned. 'Kind of. I said I freaked out because of the wasps, didn't know *where* I was going and accidentally ran *towards* the danger. They believed that . . . I think. After the bee beard thing that doesn't make much sense, but, hey, everyone knows wasps are eeeeevil!' She giggled, crinkling the large pale sticking plaster across her right cheek. 'Of course I'm grounded *forever*. I told Mum we'd made friends at concert rehearsals and asked her to drop me off here. She'll be back in an hour. I'm *never* going to be allowed to walk anywhere on my own again!'

Elena laughed. 'You seem like your old self, anyway.'

'I'm OK,' said Tima, settling into the corner of the sofa. 'Although there are some things I'd like to forget. I feel OK today. Lily phoned me up again.' She shuddered. 'If I get any more fake sympathy from her I'm going to projectile vomit up the wall!'

Elena gave a hoot of laughter and winced. Her wounds still hurt a bit.

'So . . . no more dark-light god,' said Tima. 'And you seem to have a thing going with a vampire . . . but . . . we saved this town. They'll never say thanks, but *we* saved them. You, me, and Matt.'

'And Spin,' said Elena.

'Hmm, maybe,' admitted Tima. 'Perhaps it's a good thing I didn't blow a hole in him. Matt's not going to like it, though, if you big up Spin.'

There was a ping. Elena grinned and held up her phone. 'Speaking of which . . .'

The text message on it read:

Got my phone back from Dad. Him and Mum in meltdown thinking I was nearly blown up. Left hospital this morning. Bandages really itchy. Talk tonight? Usual place and time?

CHAPTER 49

They met once more at the bandstand to share their versions of that momentous night, sitting down on the wooden floor in the moonlight, passing around their tales and filling in all the gaps.

It seemed like weeks since they'd last been there, rather than just a few nights. Matt had his left arm in a sling, seven stitches in his forehead and some impressive bandages on his legs, covering deep grazes and cuts.

'Hit some concrete. Broke my elbow, fractured my skull, and ripped some skin off,' he said, shrugging. 'Could've been worse.'

'It looks really painful,' said Elena, reaching towards his arm.

He hastily stepped back. 'It's fine if you don't touch me!' He looked from Elena to Tima. 'So . . . what now? Is it all over? Do we go back to normal?'

Lucky landed on the balustrade of the bandstand with a click of her claws. 'Normal?' she said.

'Define normal,' said Elena.

'I don't think we could be normal if we tried—not now,' said Matt, holding out his fist and smiling as Lucky landed on it. 'Tima's still playing with insects. You're still chatting to dogs and foxes, I bet. We're all still waking up.'

'Vampire boy's still out there somewhere, thirsting for you,' said Tima, as Elena rolled her eyes and shoved her.

'And I've got Lucky,' Matt concluded. He laughed and looked away, suddenly self-conscious. 'Actually—I mean that. I *have* got lucky. These last couple of weeks have been the best time of my life.'

'We were nearly *killed* by a dark-light god!' said Elena. 'How lucky is that?'

Tima grinned and pulled them both into a hug, ignoring Matt's whimper. Lucky flapped up above their heads, out of the way.

'You two are the best friends. The *best*,' said Tima.

'You're the best friends I ever had too,' said Elena.

'I'm in pain,' said Matt.

Pain, thought Spin, deep in the shadows. *You don't know what pain is. One day I'll show you.*

ALI SPARKES

Ali Sparkes was a journalist and BBC broadcaster until she chucked in the safe job to go dangerously freelance and try her hand at writing comedy scripts. Her first venture was as a comedy columnist on BBC Radio 4's *Woman's Hour* and later on *Home Truths*. Not long after, she discovered her real love was writing children's fiction.

Ali grew up adoring adventure stories about kids who mess about in the woods and still likes to mess about in the woods herself whenever possible. She lives with her husband, two sons, and a barmy labradoodle in Southampton, England.

ACKNOWLEDGEMENTS

Many thanks to Dr Simon Boxall for helpful earth science discussions (it's not over yet!) and to Sam Taylor and Claire Taylor for brilliant insights into what makes Spin roll the way he does. More on this later . . .

Thanks also, to my brilliant editor, Liz Cross, for keeping the faith after my first trashed deadline . . . and the second . . . and believing I would hit the third.

HAVE YOU READ THEM ALL?

THE SHAPESHIFTER

Ready for more incredible adventures? Try these!

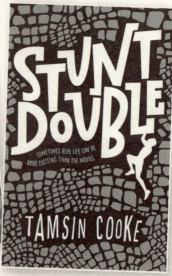